Spider

Spider

Linda Strachan

To WHEC.
Have a wild Run
With Spider!
Linda Strachan

Published by
Strident Publishing Ltd
22 Strathwhillan Drive
The Orchard, Hairmyres
East Kilbride G75 8GT

Tel: +44 (0)1355 220588
info@stridentpublishing.co.uk
www.stridentpublishing.co.uk

A catalogue record for this book is
available from the British Library.

978-1-905537-06-8

Designed by Sallie Moffat
Cover image © the earlybird, 2008
Printed by Creative Print and Design

For Stuart, Graeme and Cara

Linda Strachan

had her first (and only) flying lesson in a small plane when she was a teenager, but decided she preferred to keep her feet on the ground. Unfortunately she failed her driving test twice, possibly because the chap testing her thought she was trying to drive her Mini like a rally car. This may have been because she spent most of her time following her boyfriend to watch rallies or drive his own rally car.

Before becoming a writer she worked as a model, a medical lab technician and a fashion buyer. She likes dogs, painting pictures on walls, artichokes, olives and chocolate, but prefers writing to almost anything else.

Acknowledgements

Research for this book has taken me to all sorts of interesting places and I have met many fascinating people, who have been incredibly helpful.

My particular thanks to Andrew Kerr and Karen Macaulay – Scottish Ambulance Service, South East Division and also to Dahrlene and Ian, the Paramedic crew who allowed me to shadow them on a shift as an observer; to Colin McNeil, Colin Malcolm and Ian Stevens – Lothian and Borders Police; to Andy Gunn and Steven – Rural and Urban Training Scheme (RUTS) in Midlothian; and to the officers and trainees of the Scottish Fire Services College, Gullane, East Lothian, for allowing me to watch one of their training events. My thanks also to Joel Symonds, Megan Jankowski and Scott Lindsay and of course to my agents Kathryn and Lindsey and to Keith, Graham, Alison and Sallie at Strident.

As always I am indebted to my family, for their medical expertise and keen critical eye, and as always to my husband, Stuart, for his eternal patience and support when I am writing...and when I am not!

–Linda Strachan

CHAPTER ONE

Spider

How did I get here?

Dreams..? Nightmares, more like.

My life was sorted. Well, I thought so – I was pretty stupid. Ducking and diving here and there, thieving – just small things, twocking the odd car for a Run. A real peach of a girlfriend – rich too – and I had a reputation as a bit of a hard man. What more could I ask?

Some might say I got *exactly* what I was asking for and maybe they're right.

I just don't know or care anymore. Thought I was so clever; but you can't hide from some things and when your nightmares come true....

I had one last night. A nightmare. I didn't sleep much, so it must have been in one of those moments when you just drift off. But it was so bad I woke up screaming silently, shaking and sweating, tears streaming from my eyes, not sure where I was.

But that's probably not surprising, is it?

It was shadowy and dark in my nightmare and I was looking at Deanna. She was crying and I couldn't get her to stop. There was something in her arms but she wouldn't let me see it. Her hand was covering it and when she lifted her hand for a moment it was dripping with dark red blood. She started yelling at me.

"See what you did, Spider!"

I wanted to shout back that I didn't do it; I didn't mean it to happen. I wanted to tell her that I was sorry, so sorry....

I couldn't bear to look at what she had been hiding. I knew it would be horrible so I turned away from her. Cold shivers started running down my back. I knew I had to look - I couldn't just ignore her crying. I turned back but she had gone.

A body was lying on a bed, covered with a white sheet. My stomach churned, oily and cold as I slowly lifted the corner of the sheet.

There it was - blood, smashed bone and torn flesh - it didn't even look like a face anymore. It was broken and bloody. I knew who it was, I recognised the t-shirt.

It had been his favourite.

That was when I started screaming. I screamed so hard that my throat was sore when I woke up. But I must have been screaming in my dream because no one seemed to have heard me.

I was hoping that everything that happened had been part of the nightmare, but then I realised it was all still waiting for me.

I wish it had all been a dream, just a nightmare. I want it all to be back the way it was, but it never will be.

Some nightmares come true.

I just want it all to go away.

I don't like heights normally but this is different, a solution.

The ground is a long drop away.

CHAPTER TWO

On Friday nights Bernie's always attracted a noisy crowd, clustered on the pavement waiting to get inside, bouncers standing large and heavy at the door.

They heard it coming even before the headlights lit up the street. The throaty growl filling the air followed by the screech of punished tyres as the car tore around the corner of Maitland Street, shining sleek and black in the streetlights. Heavy drumbeats thumped from the speakers, vibrating through the night air.

Leaning out of the window, Spider gestured with his free hand, fighting for control of the mechanical beast with the other. Deanna opened her window and yelled some obscenity but the three boys in the back seat drowned her out.

Spider gunned the engine and they roared off down the road; past the closed shops and local shopping mall, along the deserted market place and down The Avenue where the cafes and bistros buzzed.

Excited by the feel of the wheel beneath his hands and the power in his control, Spider felt invincible. This was what he loved. He could do anything, be anything.

At end of the street a couple of kids were standing by the side of the road. They stood frozen in the headlights like rabbits. Spider spun the wheel with the palm of his hand and thrust his foot hard down on the accelerator. The wheels screeched as the car fought back and he grabbed the steering wheel with both hands.

The back end hung out and Spider felt the wheels skid on the slick road. Just as the tyres gripped the road again he thought he felt a thump against the back of the car. A momentary flash of panic swept through him. Had he hit those kids? One of them looked about the same age as Benny. The others hadn't noticed anything and he realised it must have been the tyres bumping the kerb. Pedal down, the engine roared and trying to control the monster as it leapt onwards banished all other thoughts from his mind.

Deanna's hands gripped the sides of her seat, knuckles white as they pressed through the skin, her body rigid and her face in a rictus grin as they swung around another tight corner. She would never admit to being afraid. Spider had said he wasn't going to do it any more, that they would put him away for months this time if he got caught, but Deanna had been desperate to go out with them. She had so often listened to the boys talking about the cars they took. She wanted to see what it was like, feel the thrill of doing something so wild, and she knew Spider wouldn't refuse her.

She wanted to 'twock a car'. She loved the way Spider said it and she almost managed the accent, but she was wary of saying it in front of him and his mates because she was sure her cultured vowels would sneak through and make them laugh at her.

She had watched them tearing through the town in stolen cars. It looked so incredible. She wanted to feel the thrill of it all, to be part of it, one of the gang. Finally she had persuaded Spider to take her along, although Deanna knew Andy wasn't happy about her being there at all.

Andy grabbed the back of Spider's seat. His tense, excited expression showed that the buzz had started to rise through him. He would rather have been up in front with Spider, as usual, but Spider had insisted that she should get the front seat. At first he had been tempted to tell Spider he wasn't coming but Spider gave him that look – and as always Andy backed down. What Spider said went, that was how it was, how it had always been.

The street lights whipped past as they raced down the dark streets of the town, lurching into corners and thumping over dips in the road. Spider hollered each time they slewed into a corner, and they all joined in.

At the top of Tor Hill they drew to a stop at the traffic lights. A flash sports car drew in beside them.

"Race 'im!" Joe screeched from the back.

"Yeah, Spider" Baz shrieked, "We can take 'im."

The driver of the sports car looked over at them so Baz and Andy howled, and gave him the finger.

Spider watched the traffic lights, revving the car ready for the take off. He glanced at the other driver and revved some more. The red light was steady, un-changing, but Spider knew it would go any minute now. He felt the car rear up against the handbrake, making the others yell louder.

At last the lights changed and slowly releasing the clutch, Spider kept the revs high so that the wheels started to spin and scream. The smell of burning rubber filled his nostrils as the car shuddered and pounced forwards leaving the other far behind. Andy looked out the back window but the sports car was turning off, down a side street.

"Chicken!" Andy howled at the driver.

Tor Hill was a long steep straight stretch of road that shone ahead of them, outlined by the yellow street-lights, bright as a ribbon in the moonlight. At the foot of the hill was the police station. Another buzz. Getting the bizzies to chase them upped the ante.

"Faster. Move it!" urged Andy.

"Yeah, go for it, Spider!" shouted Joe.

Spider put his foot down hard on the accelerator.

"Ya wee beauty!" Andy grinned as the car took off and the engine growled as it rocketed faster down the hill, gaining speed all the time. The passing gardens became a blur of shadows. Spider's howls and Andy's shrieks reverberated inside the car. Joe, Baz and Deanna added to the cacophony with screams of their own.

The car was an arrow whipping through the night air. They were ace, and invincible.

They reached the foot of the hill but there was no one about. One solitary police car sat unoccupied in the dark police station car park. Not much chance of a chase there.

Andy leaned over Spider's shoulder and held his hand on the horn. It wailed though the quiet night.

"Let's do the Parse!" Baz leaned forwards between the front seats.

"Yeah, Spider." Andy nudged Baz out of the way. He and Spider grinned at each other. "The Parse!" they chorused.

Parsehill Lane was their place, a series of garages that wound its way behind the older houses. It was a complicated warren of twisting alleyways, which linked the various blocks of lock-ups.

Known as a safe meeting place, The Parse was a maze of hiding places and dead ends. Every now and then, when the local residents complained enough, the police came and tried to clear out the gangs and pushers who inhabited its dark corners. But it was no easy task with a myriad of exits and escape routes, so within a day or two it was back to business as usual.

The road that led to The Parse was a wide curve that swept along the front of the housing estate and past the playing fields behind. Driving at speed through The Parse was one of the greatest challenges, not just because it was a narrow twisting lane, but because there were always new obstacles, a motorbike or even a burnt out car hiding around a corner to trap the unwary.

Spider stopped the car for a moment gathering his thoughts for the Run. Once he had started the clock would be ticking and he had to get right through in a oner, he had a reputation to uphold.

Andy glared at Baz as he started to speak, Spider had to concentrate. Deanna silently watched Spider.

He was sitting with his eyes closed, psyching himself up for the Run, hands gripping the steering wheel fiercely. It was all part of the showmanship; make them wait - he was in control.

After a couple of long quiet minutes of anticipation Spider opened his eyes and revved the car. The others gave a yell.

"Hold on," Spider growled. "For the ride of your life!"

Gripping the wheel he slowly lifted his foot off the clutch, the smell of burning rubber filling the car once more as the wheels screamed their torture. Whooping loudly Spider fought to keep it under control, sensing the exact moment to let the car have its head. The tyres fought for traction on the road, finally propelling the car into The Parse.

Deanna held her breath. She grabbed onto the dashboard. The headlights lit up the first wall and it loomed threateningly close as the car turned into the dark alley. Spider spun the wheel but the long concrete wall seemed to go on forever. He screwed up his face in anticipation of the crunch, but the car kept on turning, its wheels hugging the road until the narrow alley yawned open before them.

He knew the bends and turns in The Parse off by heart, every inch of it was familiar territory and he knew exactly where he could shave a few seconds off the Run. He was the best.

First right, then left, gathering speed on the short straight. A hairpin left then left again. Spider felt a surge of adrenalin. The corkscrew was coming next, a dangerous wavering, curving alley that narrowed before ending in a sharp right.

"Watch that bike!" Andy yelled.

The hideous scrape of metal as the car caught the side of the motorbike and sent it spinning across the road behind them. Spider stood on the brakes as they thundered towards the right-hand turn. The tyres squealed leaving behind a hot slick of rubber on the road. The back of the car smashed against the wall on Deanna's side and they were all thrown sideways, but Spider accelerated and the monster jumped forwards fearlessly towards the next hazard.

Bracing one arm against the door Deanna tried to find a handhold. She dug her nails into the leather seat beneath her and pushed herself back against the seat.

The Parse opened out for a few hundred yards. Spider gunned it down the open stretch. They turned into the second twisting alleyway, wheels spinning as the car fought for traction. The road was a little wider here and Spider got up more speed as his confidence soared.

He blasted the horn as they approached three shadowy figures standing in their path. All three dived for the side and flattened themselves against a garage door their mouths open in soundless shrieks of shock and abuse.

Joe, Baz and Andy yelled back at them scornfully but Spider was focusing on the road ahead. The next part was tricky. A series of garages were set stepped out into the road along the next corner. There was plenty of room if you were driving slowly, but at speed it was like chicanes. Spider wove the car in and out of the buildings glancing off the corner of one with a screech of protesting metal as the stonework scored the side of the car. He regained control as they came out of the corner and into the next narrow alley.

Someone had placed a skip at the side of their lock-up and metal rods were sticking out of the top like giant skewers. A couple of them jutted into their path and Deanna instinctively ducked as the car squeezed under them and they scraped across the roof of the car with a noise like dark shrieks of pain.

Spider gasped a breath of relief. That had been close.

A moment's lapse of concentration and he realised he was approaching the next corner too fast. It was a sharp right-hand turn followed by a hairpin left.

He stood on the brakes and fought with the wheel.

Deanna grabbed the dashboard, grimacing as she was flung from side to side. Protesting yelps came from the back of the car as Spider tore the wheel first one way then the other.

"We're going too fast!" Andy yelled, his pale face appearing between the seats. "We'll never make it."

"Yes, we will!" Spider growled back at him, teeth clenched, willing it to be true. His words were barely tasting the air before he realised Andy might be right.

They were almost out of the bend when the car caught the corner of a wall and started to spin out of control. The windscreen was filled with the huge, dark and impenetrable wall ahead. Spider struggled to keep hold of the steering wheel, trying to accelerate out of trouble but it twisted out of his hands and spun of its own accord. They hit the wall sideways with a hard crunch, slewed back across the road and bounced wildly from side to side, their speed making everything blur.

A dislodged metal bin rolled across the road in front of the car. Catching it side on, the car rose up riding over the bin, tilting wildly as it ploughed on. Screaming tyres and roaring engine noise shred the air until the car slammed down to skid along on its side. The screech of tearing metal filled the car as it scraped along the road, crunching and rattling like an avalanche, metal side panels mutilated by the road's surface. Still hurtling forward at the ferocious rate of an express train, the sleek, black bonnet of the car crunched and flattened out against the wall in front of it. The back end rose in the air tossing its passengers around like rag dolls. Deanna was thrown into the air and then back down hard against the passenger door and with a bang the two front airbags inflated.

Baz bounced up hitting the roof while Andy was catapulted forward between the front seats, through the windscreen towards the wall.

Still on its side, the car settled back down onto the ground with a final crash, The metal-crunching cacophony suddenly stopped, leaving an eerie silence that was broken only by the monotonous sound of the car horn howling into the still night.

CHAPTER THREE

Spider

I'm still alive!

At least I think I am.

Something's wrong. Above me I can see a broken window, spears of glass cutting into the night sky. It takes a few minutes to shrug off the dazed feeling before I realise I'm lying all scrunched up. At first I don't even think about moving. The car is lying on its side and the horn is blaring, a whining, irritating sound that just goes on and on.

Everything is weird. I try to understand it. Down is the passenger side of the car and up is the driver's window with its broken shards of glass. It's pretty dark inside the car with just a shaft of moonlight filtering through and I can see the squashed remains of an air bag in front of me, I always wondered what they looked like. It's collapsed, but because I'd been thrown sideways I must have missed the bag almost entirely.

A fine white powder covers my hands and what I can see of my clothes. It rises, like smoke in the air as I breathe. There's a sharp nagging pain in my foot, and my chest hurts but I have no inclination to move, not yet, anyway. I try to think straight but the continuing whining lament of the horn makes it difficult to concentrate.

A cough and a groan come from the back of the car.

"Andy? Is that you?" I move my leg as I speak and a white hot flash of pain tears the breath from my throat. With a struggle I try to get up but there's something soft beneath me. With a shudder I realise it's Deanna and she isn't moving or making a sound. I try to pull myself off her, grabbing the steering wheel but that makes my chest hurt. I have to keep my right foot as steady as I can to stop the pain that stabs all the way up my leg every time I move.

The windscreen is smashed and there is nothing left but crumbled crystals around the edges. Deanna, slumped down between the passenger seat and the floor, is lying crumpled half against the door. She's still not moving. The side window below her is shattered and I can just make out splinters of glass sticking in her hair as they catch the moonlight.

There is scuffling and swearing from the back. Someone is clambering about and all I can see is a collection of arms and legs. I can't turn round to see much.

"Sheeeit!" Joe appears between the seats for a moment, his pale face catching the light. He's got a streak of blood across his cheek where he's smeared it with his hand. "I think my arm's broken!" he whines.

"Don't be a wimp, Joe," Baz sneers climbing across him. "If it was broken you wouldn't be able to move it. I'm gettin' out."

With a lot of grumbling and swearing Baz and Joe climb out of the glass encrusted hole that had been the rear window. I try to move again. A piercing pain shoots up my leg when I move my foot. It's stuck and every movement is agony. I realise I'm trapped in the car. The horn is still drilling its whine into my head.

"Joe, where's Andy?" I shout at the leg that is disappearing rapidly out of the back window.

"Shit!" Joe curses again as he joins Baz. I can just see the top of their heads as they hobble about in front of the car looking down at the ground.

"He's had it! Oh shit!" I can hear Joe puking.

"Christ! What a mess. I'm off. Let's get the hell out, Joe," Baz growls.

"Come back!" I yell at them as they run off. "You useless…" I wipe my eyes clear of tears of helplessness and frustration.

I'm stuck here. What if the petrol ignites and the car starts to burn? I can't get out! I struggle to move but I can't do anything, I'm really stuck.

What if…what if it…?

I've got to get out!

I know I'm beginning to lose it completely. I've got to stop this and try to think straight.

If only the car wasn't on its side. I just want the horn to stop, the noise is driving me crazy. I can't think.

A cloud moves across the sky and a bright shaft of moonlight lights up the inside of the car so that I get a proper look at Deanna's face. She's unconscious and there's blood on her face. I realise that even if I could get out she would still be stuck in the car.

She's crammed into a small space almost beneath me and she looks pretty bad but she's still breathing, giving short shallow gasps. That stops me for a moment as I realise what I had been thinking and it gets through to my befuddled brain. Deanna is breathing now, but what if she stopped?

Shit! What a mess.

Where's Andy?

"Andy!" I yell as loud as I can, frantically, abov[...]
the horn. I stretch to try and see between the seats,[...]
seat is empty and the pain steals my breath again.

"Oh, bloody hell!" I groan, as my stomach plumm[...] [...]
I gasp for breath but all the air seems to have drained from my
lungs.

Why doesn't the horn stop? I can't think with that noise bor-
ing right through me and it just goes on and on. My leg hurts so
much that when I try to move it I almost pass out.

Deanna's still not moving and I'm not sure if I'm crushing her
by leaning on her, but there is nothing I can do about it. I don't
want to begin to think about Andy.

Surely someone should have heard the horn by now, but maybe no one would bother. There has been a lot of trouble in the
Parse in the last few months and none of the locals would come
down here at night.

I wish I still had a mobile phone but my dad smashed it in one
of his rages and I've not done anything about getting another
one.

A thought sparks in my head. I don't have a phone, but Deanna
does.

In the dismal light I squint to try and see where her bag is and
I can just see something pale lying beside her foot. It's at the far
side of the foot well, almost further than my fingers can reach.
I start to stretch past her to get closer, trying to ignore the sickening pain that makes me come out in a cold sweat whenever I
move my leg.

After what seems like an eternity, stretching inch by inch my
fingertips reach the strap of Deanna's bag. I feel a sharp sting in

...y shoulder as I push that extra bit to get my fingertips around it. Pulling it towards me, I wedge myself once more between Deanna and the side of the seat so that I don't fall back onto her again.

Rummaging about inside her bag my fingers feel the familiar shape and a wave of relief floods through me as they curl around her phone. I wish I had a little more light but the clouds have moved again, covering the moon — making everything even darker than before.

Pulling the phone out of her bag I can see the signal registering as strong.

I dial 999.

The operator sounds calm. "What service do you require?"

"Send an ambulance, quickly! The car's crashed and I think Andy's..." I can't say the word.

"Just one moment caller."

"Ambulance service."

A new voice comes on the line. "Can you confirm your telephone number?"

"I don't know the number. It's not my phone. We need an ambulance Deanna's hurt and.."

"One moment caller...Now, can you tell me the exact location of the incident?"

"We've crashed, we're in the Parse and we..."

"The Parse? I need to know where that is. The ambulance needs to know where to go. Can you tell me the exact address?

"No, I don't know the address." I groan. Everyone locally knows the Parse it was just one of those places - you knew where it was. I'd never thought about it having an address.

"Are there any landmarks you can give me? What is around you?"

My mind goes blank. I can't think of anything. "It's just the Parse, they're lock-ups. Behind the houses…"

I think of something. "It's behind the Slackton playing fields."

"That's fine, caller, I have the location. Now would you confirm it for me. The Parsehill Lane lock-ups behind the Slackton Playing fields?"

"Yes. That's it."

"Fine, the ambulance will be with you shortly. Now, what's your name?"

"Spider."

"Okay Spider," her voice begins to sound softer. "How old are you?"

"…Fifteen."

"Can you tell me what happened?"

"The car crashed and it's on its side. My girlfriend, Deanna, she's not moving…I think it's bad. There's blood on her head, a lot of it. It's all over her face and dripping in her eyes. I ended up lying on top of her and I can't get up properly - the car's on its side." I know I'm gabbling on but I can't seem to help it.

"I thought I'd killed her. I don't know what to do. Andy's gone. I think he might be outside but I can't see. I think he's dead." My voice breaks and disappears up three octaves. "They just stood there staring at something on the ground. It must be Andy. Andy isn't in the car any more. They just ran off and left us and…"

"Spider." The operator's calm voice interrupts me. "You'll have to calm down if you want to help Deanna."

I know I must sound like a right idiot. "Sorry, sorry! I don't know what to do, you've got to come, you've got to. Come and get me!"

"All right, Spider. Are you still in the car?"

"Yeah, I'm stuck. I think my foot's caught. It's bloody sore. I can't get it out."

"Who else is in the car?"

"Just Deanna and me. The others got out the back, but I didn't see Andy. I think he's outside. They said he'd had it!"

"Can you see if Deanna's breathing? Look and see if you can see her chest moving."

I watch Deanna for a moment or two.

"Yeah, she's breathing."

"You said she was bleeding. How badly? Is it serious bleeding, spurting out?"

"There's a lot of blood on her face and all over the place, but… no, it's not spurting out."

"Good. Now if she wakes up don't give her anything to eat or drink."

The calm voice is irritating. Where would I get anything to drink? Doesn't the woman realise we need an ambulance. Why is she chuntering on like this and not doing anything?

"Can't you just send us an ambulance?" I can hear my voice wobble as I say it.

"Spider, the ambulance has been on its way ever since you told me where you were. They'll be there very soon. I want you to watch for them and tell me when you hear them or see the lights."

"Okay."

"I need to ask you a few more questions. Can you see any obvious injuries on yourself?"

"No, it's just my foot. It only hurts when I try to move. I keep slipping sideways and that hurts. My chest hurts a bit when I breathe."

"I want you to try to stay still, don't move around, the ambulance is on its way."

A bright blue light flashes lighting up the sky behind the roof of the nearest lock-up. The light flashes again, bright and blue, the kind of thing that normally has me running for cover, but for once all I feel is a rush of relief.

"I can see the lights! I think they're here," I tell the woman.

In moments the area is bathed in flashing lights and there are lots of people in fluorescent jackets.

Help has arrived.

CHAPTER FOUR

Spider

The trolley is so hard it feels like trying to sleep on the pavement. I shift around a bit but it doesn't matter which way I turn it still makes my leg hurt. My chest is still sore and they said I've probably bruised my ribs. I feel like I've been lying here for hours, my watch is crawling past the minutes, but when I check I can see it's only been 45 minutes since they brought me into Accident and Emergency.

I can hear some doctors talking about some little kid who has come in. It was a hit and run. It reminds me of the kid I almost hit when the car hit the kerb. I know I missed him but he looked the same age as my little brother. I must be going soft but even thinking about it makes my stomach churn.

'Don't go there, mate,' a quiet inner voice whispers. 'Don't even begin to think it could have been Benny.'

Even though he is younger than Joey and Ashley, he's a really bright little kid, probably the brightest of the lot of us. He had his seventh birthday last week and I nicked a computer game for him. It was the one he had been pestering mum about for ages. Benny's eyes lit up when he saw it and he gave me one of his cheeky little grins. He's pretty smart and he told me last night he had got through to the tenth level already.

I told Mum I'd done a little part time work and earned the money to buy the game. She'd given me that look. The one she always gives me when she's sure I'm spinning her a story. My mum is as straight as they come, but time has worn away the energy to argue with me, or my dad. Dad, well, he's another story.

The doctor finally comes back and tells me I'm lucky I wasn't much worse, that most of it is just bruising. They're sending me for an x-ray so I just have to wait…wait and think. I hate that, waiting and thinking.

All I can think about is Deanna and Andy.

It seemed to take the firemen ages to get us out of the car although it probably wasn't really all that long. The ambulance had arrived with two fire engines just behind it. It was like one minute I was there on my own and the next the whole place was lit up like a circus with flashing lights and people shouting orders.

The car rocked slightly and then I heard them pushing something against it and the rocking stopped. One of the firemen came and spoke to me at the window, he said they had to get the car stabilised before they could get us out. Someone had set up some lights so for the first time I could see how bad Deanna looked. She was like a broken doll, crumpled against the side of the car where she and I had been thrown. Once the car had stopped rocking a face appeared at the front of the car, looking through the broken windscreen.

"Hi. I'm a paramedic, my name's Gary, what's yours?"

"Spider."

"Okay, Spider. I want you to keep looking straight at me and don't move or try to look around."

I could hear someone coming into the car from the back window.

"That's right, Spider," Gary said. "Just look straight at me, don't move your head."

Someone had crawled inside the car through the back window. Hands behind me were holding my head steady, stopping it from moving.

"This is Lucy, Spider," Gary said.

"Hello, Spider." The voice behind me was bright and cheery.

Gary nodded towards Deanna. "Is that your girlfriend?"

I tried to turn and look at her but Lucy was holding my head so that it wouldn't move. "Yeah. Her name's Deanna. She'll be all right, won't she?"

"I'm just going to check her, now."

I was still lying half on top of Deanna but Lucy was now holding my head from behind and insisting that I mustn't try to move it.

She was telling Gary things about Deanna but I didn't understand most of it. I knew that Deanna had bashed her head; I had seen a horrible slash across her forehead. I got a sudden picture of her hair flying through the air as she was being tossed about, just before the car crashed onto its side.

A fireman came over and started pushing a big flat plastic board between the windscreen and me. Then they covered us all, Lucy, Deanna and me, with a heavy sheet, which blotted out all the light. It soon became incredibly hot under the sheet.

Lucy chatted on, explaining that they put the cover over us to stop things like broken glass hitting us while the firemen removed the windscreen with huge pincers. There was a lot of noise and I had no idea what was happening most of the time but Lucy kept nattering on, explaining things to me.

"They're going to take the roof off the car, Spider," she said. "That's what all the noise is. They have to take the roof off so that we can get you and Deanna out safely."

She stayed holding my head still and talking the whole time.

"Spider's an interesting name. Is there a story behind it?" she asked.

It was difficult to concentrate with all the noise going on around me and I suppose that was why she was trying to keep my mind off it all.

"Everyone's always called me Spider," I told her. "Ever since I was a kid. I used to collect spiders, all kinds of strange ones."

"I thought it might have been something to do with Spider-man," Lucy's voice had a laugh in it. "I thought you might have been good at climbing or something."

"Not me, no way!" I shuddered. "I hate heights."

When the cover was lifted off again I could hardly believe it. The car roof had been peeled back like the top of a tin can. It looked like a convertible.

There were lots of people milling around and with the top of the car gone I could see what was going on. Gary came back and put a stiff collar around my neck to stop me moving my head.

"I'm okay," I said, but my voice wavered a bit and I sounded like a kid.

"We'll get you out of there soon, but the door is buckled so we will need to get rid of it first. I'm going to put this cover over you again, just for a bit, while they cut the door off, okay?"

The heavy sheet was pulled across us again and Lucy made sure that it covered Deanna and herself and me.

A rumbling noise droned on and on followed by a kind of slow crunch. Once…Twice…As the huge pinch cutters cut through metal posts that hold the car doors. A screeching sound of complaining metal sounded very close as they cut off the driver's door.

The cover came off again and I saw them bring a stretcher past the car. There was someone on it. It was Andy. I knew that by the jeans and the trainers with the green stripes on them and that new t-shirt that Andy was so proud of. At first all I could see was his body being carried into the back of the ambulance. There were so many people around by then that I couldn't see properly but when someone moved what little I did see of him made me want to puke.

Where Andy's face should have been was a mass of…No, I still can't think about it.

"Oh God, …" I heard a voice and it was a bit before I realised it was coming from me. Cold sweat started trickling down my back and I felt my mouth fill with water. "I think I'm going to puke…"

A handful of cloths appeared in Lucy's hands. I managed to stop myself before I puked all over everyone. That would have been really embarrassing.

"Okay, Spider, just take your time," Gary said. "Try to take some deep breaths and stay calm and we'll have you out of there in a moment."

I heard Deanna moaning but then she was quiet again. Lucy was doing something but I couldn't turn to see because of the collar.

Gary leaned down and they slipped a board beneath me so that I could be lifted out of the space where the door had been.

They carried me to the ambulance. I saw them getting Deanna out of the car just before they closed the doors, there was another ambulance waiting for her.

When they got me to the hospital I was shifted onto this trolley and left to wait for a doctor. No one seemed to be able to tell me how Deanna was, or anything about Andy.

Andy!

It makes me sick to think about him. In my head I can still see him, lying on the stretcher, a mess where his face should be.

CHAPTER FIVE

Deanna

It feels warm and sunny like the summer holiday we spent in the south of France. I float along with the pleasant thoughts of sun, sea and sand. But there is something uncomfortable, something dark and frightening hovering at the edges. I push it away. I always push things that I don't like to think about to the back of my mind. If I ignore them enough they sometimes go away.

I wish that strange ticking: that sort of bleeping noise near to my ear would go away. I should really open my eyes and see what it is but I just can't be bothered. I wish it would stop, though, it's so irritating. Bleep...bleep...bleep...

It's just the same as that security alarm that Spider set off, just to show me.

We were in this shop listening to CDs when Spider told me how he could get past security. I remember I could feel my heart thumping as I watched him sidle up to the open door, holding a CD in his hand.

The bleeping alarm started up as he reached the door. I tried to make myself smaller so that no one would notice me. Spider had that 'I can do anything and you can't stop me!' expression on his face that I know so well. It's one of the things I really love about him, and the way he always knows what he's doing. Nothing bothers him and no one, but no one, can tell him what to do. It was the same expression he wore whenever one of the teachers started giving him a hard time: on the few occasions he actually made it into school, that is.

When the security guard approached him, Spider shrugged and waved the CD about in front of him and started making gestures. The security guard said a few words then moved on. Spider came wandering back and swapped that CD for another one.

I knew this was my moment to move and when Spider moved towards the door again I wandered over as casually as I could to the door. It was horrible but exciting at the same time. I felt as though my heart was doing somersaults and everyone in the shop was looking at me. I kept my eyes glued to the floor. I was gripping my bag tight against my side, hoping that no one would see the stolen CD inside. I felt as though my new handbag was completely transparent and everyone could see a flashing sign on my forehead that said 'Guilty'.

I heard my cue and when the security bleeps went off again Spider made a huge fuss about apologising to the guard and fooling around as I slipped out of the shop.

The last few steps onto the street were the

most difficult because my legs had turned to water. I scurried along the road and around the corner shaking and waiting for the heavy hand on my shoulder that meant I had been caught.

The stupid thing was I didn't really want the CD and I felt so guilty about it that I threw it away in the end. I never told Spider. I didn't want him to think I was pathetic. He is so cool, so in control. Nothing seems to bother him and nobody tells him what to do. I wish I was like that.

I never told him about the other thing either. I wanted to but I'm worried that he'll tell me to go away, that it's not his problem, but I can't tell anyone else either and I don't know what to do.

I don't even want to think about it but it keeps on popping into my head so that I can't think of anything else. What if my parents find out?

I can just see their faces. My mother will crack up and my dad...They'll both say it's all Spider's fault. They didn't want me to have anything to do with him. But Spider makes me feel so alive. He always knows what to do and he looks after me. No one says a thing to me when Spider's around. None of them would dare call me names, or give me a hard time. Spider understands me more than my parents, with their high-class, high-powered lives and all their fancy friends; they have no idea what it is like for me.

Spider makes things feel right.

Anyway it might never happen. It could all be a mistake, but deep down I know it's not a mistake, it is really happening and I should have told him about it.

I wish Spider and I could go away somewhere warm and sunny. Maybe we could go on a holiday somewhere. I could take him to that place in France we went on holiday last year, and we could go swimming and go for long walks along a warm sandy beach as the sun sets all wonderful colours. Or we could just lie on the beach together. I can feel it. I am floating on the water, drifting and floating, drifting and floating.

CHAPTER SIX

Andy

Yeah, well, I thought I was blind at first, didn't I! Everything hurt, especially when they tried to lift me off the ground. The last thing I remember was the horrible noise when we hit the wall and being thrown across the car. I thought that was it, I was a gonner, but the car just kept on going, screaming metal crunching as it careered along the ground.

I was thrown on top of Baz and Joe who were yelling and screaming, goin' off their heads. I couldn't believe the car didn't stop. It screeched, scraping along the road on its side and the noise just went on and on, forever. Then we hit something and I was thrown up into the air and that was it. I've tried but I can't remember anything else until I heard all the noise and sirens and folk around me.

I was sure I was blind because I couldn't see anything except a red haze and my eyes felt glued together. At first I couldn't remember where I was. I thought I had been asleep and dreaming some kind of nightmare, then I began to wonder if I was dead.

That was before the pain started. Red-hot needles jabbing into my face and eyes. I tried to open my mouth to scream but it didn't seem to work. There was a grotty hot metallic taste in my mouth and it was a while before my brain recognised it as blood.

There hadn't been any blood when Fiona died.

She looked like she had no blood in her at all when they got her out. Her skin had turned a strange kind of grey colour. That was because of the water, they said.

I'd never seen a dead body before. It still looked a bit like Fiona, but it didn't, sort of like a doll with Fiona's face.

Oh, God! Mum and dad!

They'll be furious with me for this. It seems like everything I do makes them more miserable. This will just make mum look at me with that awful sad expression she gets a lot of the time, ever since Fiona.

At first I used to try and do things for them, to make them happy to say, 'Look at me I'm still here, I'm still alive!' Nothing seemed to make any difference, except that they never want me to go and do anything that might be dangerous or make them worry about me.

Like the time I wanted to go on that holiday trip with the school. Everyone else was going. They sounded like they were trying to be reasonable but I gave in pretty quickly and said I wouldn't go. I didn't want them to go back over Fiona and all that, because they might start asking awkward questions and then they might find out what really happened.

I tried to open my eyes in the ambulance but I

couldn't. When I tried to speak to ask if I was blind, it just came out as a croak and a groan and they said they had put something over my eyes and I was to try to lie still. My voice sounded strange and trying to talk hurt my mouth so it was easier to do as they said.

I wanted to ask them about Spider. He's my best mate, has been since ever. We do everything together. But things have been different since Deanna came along. I don't see why she has to come out with us all the time; she's just a girl.

Pretty cool looking, I suppose. Not my type though, I prefer blondes. I suppose she's okay, most of the time, not like most girls. Just one thing, though, she's always trying to prove she's one of us, but underneath it she thinks she's better than everyone else. But ever since Spider stopped those nerds from Hapfields calling her names she's latched onto him, getting in the way and wanting Spider to take her everywhere.

Like tonight - Spider's never taken a girl on a Run before. Said it was her idea, probably was, he knew his social worker told him that if he got caught on a Run again he'd be sent down and Spider didn't want that. If he's not there who's going to look out for his mum and his brothers and wee sister when his dad gets a skinful and starts to beat them up?

Deanna seems to be able to make Spider do whatever she wants. Nothing scares her but I reckon that's probably because her parents are rich and she knows they would save their precious daughter if she got into trouble. They could afford to buy her way out of just about anything.

Spider sticks up for her all the time; he even had a go at me when he thought I didn't want her around because I didn't like her.

He couldn't see that it was because she's a GIRL and she's always around, getting in the way, wanting Spider to go off and do other things with her. He wants to spend all his time with her now. There was a time when we spent all our time together. Spider and me - that was just how it was, best mates, always.

All the way to the hospital they were giving me injections and doing things to my face. I ignored them most of the time, unless they asked me if I was okay, like when it really hurt. I wasn't impressed when they started to cut off my jeans and T-shirt. That was my best gear!

By the time my brain had processed exactly what they were doing it was too late to do anything, but I couldn't talk anyway because they put a mask on my face. The paramedic told me it was oxygen, and boy was it good stuff! Like breathing fresh, cold air; like off a mountain or something.

When we stopped they pushed the trolley down a ramp and it seemed to take ages. All I could hear was the wheels rumbling along. When they moved me off the trolley every bit of me hurt. I yelped but it turned into a scream when they shifted my legs.

It was like someone had sliced through me with a white-hot sword.

There seems to be a lot of people talking all around me, in those serious but urgent voices they use in all the hospital programs on the telly. I don't care what happens. I just feel like every bit of me is hurting and I want it all to stop.

I'll be fine, though, just as long as they don't put me under. If I talk when I'm asleep I might spew it all out, all about Fiona. Mum and Dad would never forgive me, then.

Why can't they just leave me alone, I'm tired.

I want to ask them what happened to Spider but I can't speak, I can't say anything. Spider was in the front and in all those things on the telly about accidents; it's usually the ones in the front that get wiped. I can't imagine Spider not being there. He's indestructible, I hope. Oh God, I hope I don't start to blubber.

I try to tell them that I don't want to go under with an anaesthetic. No one will let me even try to speak. I just have to lie here while they do whatever they want and hope they won't knock me out.

"Please, please, just give me a break, Doc, let me stay awake. Please!"

I try to grunt and tell them but they just keep on shushing me and saying my parents will be here soon.

God! What a mess.

CHAPTER SEVEN

PC David Hilton sighed and took a look at his watch. Just past midnight. This was going to be a long night.

He pulled aside the curtain. Spider was sitting up on the bed looking sorry for himself, but Hilton felt little sympathy for the lad. He had hoped his last warning had sunk in but tonight's disaster was fair evidence that it had done little to change his ways.

"Well, Spider?"

Spider looked up and a wave of relief crossed his face as he realised it was someone he knew, even if it was 'Heartless Hilton' as all the local kids called him. Being all on his own had left him with far too much time to think about what had happened.

Spider actually liked Davy Hilton, not that he'd ever admit it to anyone. He knew Hilton was always straight with him but he had made Spider promise he wouldn't be doing any more Runs, ever again.

Spider stared down at the covers.

Hilton stood at the end of his bed. "I thought you were going to give this up?"

Spider shrugged and turned his head away.

"Your dad's on his way."

"Shit."

"You know the score. Did you think this would all just go away? That no one would do anything about it? You could all have been killed. The other parents are coming in, too. You've really done it this time."

"I didn't mean…They won't tell me how Deanna is." Spider screwed up his face. "I saw them take Andy away. It was horrible. No one will tell me anything!" Spider's voice broke and he coughed to cover it. "I can't help thinking about Andy." Spider looked bleakly at Hilton. "He was my best mate, always joking and messing around, thought he was another Billy Connolly.

'I can't believe I'll never see him again. I killed him. I didn't mean…I didn't mean…any of it."

Hilton frowned. "Andy's not dead, Spider. He's hurt, pretty messed up, but he's not dead."

Spider stared blankly, disbelieving. "He's not dead?"

Hilton shook his head. "He's in a bad way, though," Hilton said.

"But he isn't dead?" Spider needed to hear Hilton say it again.

"No, he's going to need a lot of fixing up, but he isn't dead."

"He is going to be okay, though, isn't he?"

"His injuries don't seem to be life threatening but it will be a while before he's out of hospital."

"What about Deanna? Is she okay? Can I see her?"

Hilton looked at Spider seeing a different look on the boy's face when he talked about Deanna. He'd seen her with Spider a couple of times and remembered thinking she didn't seem his type, too high class, but you never could tell.

"We're waiting for her parents to come in. She's still unconscious but they say she's stable. That's all they're saying just now, but I don't think you will be able to see her too soon."

Spider turned away and Hilton gave him a moment or two to compose himself.

"How are you?"

Spider shrugged again. "Mostly cuts and bruises but they don't know about my foot yet. I've to go for an x-ray. They say my ribs are just bruised but it hurts like hell when I breathe."

There was a commotion in the corridor beyond the curtain. A gruff voice, none too steady and ready for an argument by the sound of it, was harassing the nurses.

Spider closed his eyes and clenched his fists. He would recognise that voice anywhere. Now the circus was about to begin. Whenever his life took a turn for the worse his father seemed to arrive and compound it. It seemed tonight was no exception.

Hilton recognised the voice, too. Taking a deep breath he slipped out of the cubicle.

"Where is he, the little shit?" growled a burly figure.

He was not exactly staggering but a porter was following behind him, ready to act the moment things looked like turning ugly. Hilton gave the man a nod and went to intercept Spider's father before he caused an incident.

"Mr Greene? We've met before. I'm PC Hilton, the Youth Liaison Officer. Could I have a word with you?"

The sight of the police uniform got through to the man's alcohol-soaked brain quicker than anything Hilton actually said. Spider's father stood straighter for a moment. This brought him face to face with Hilton who tried not to breathe as a gust of overpoweringly foul breath filled the air between them.

"Hilton? Yeah, I remember you. Not a lot of use, are you? Never stopped the little shit trying to kill folk, have you?"

"Perhaps we could have a word in private, Sir?" Hilton took the man's arm and guided him towards a side room.

Spider heaved a sigh of relief. He would have to confront his father soon but even a short respite was welcome.

"Andy's not dead!" A grin began to work its way onto his face but it didn't last long.

CHAPTER EIGHT

Spider

A male nurse comes to take me to X-ray and tells Dad that he can wait, if he wants to. Dad gives the nurse a mouthful and goes off, muttering something about having better things to do. I never thought I would be pleased to be waiting around in a wheelchair, but anything is better than listening to my old man moaning at me non-stop.

The nurse calls after him to tell him he should wait in the waiting room until a decision is made as to whether they are going to send me home or not. I hear him cursing and swearing as he staggers off in the direction the nurse had shown him.

All through the questions Davey Hilton had asked me earlier, Dad couldn't help putting his oar in, saying things like 'You stupid little jerk. Wait until I get you home, I'll sort you out.'

I told him to bugger off and it was only the fact that Hilton was sitting beside him that stopped him from thumping me there and then. I was banking on that.

One of these days I'm going to lose my head with him again. I remember the first time I stood up to him last year. Mum had scrimped and saved to get the little ones the things they wanted for Christmas. She had taken on some extra work cleaning and was worn out. I tried to help out but she didn't want me to get her stuff by thieving so there wasn't much else I could do.

It was the day after Christmas. There was a film on and mum

had got us all fish and chips. I had been planning to go out later to find Andy and the rest but it was only half past eight.

Whether he had been thrown out of the pub or had got himself into a fight we never found out, but whatever it was he was pretty far gone.

The front door crashed open and I could hear him thumping off the walls as he tried to get down the hallway. The door flew open and he leaned against the wall.

"Whatcha' doin'?"

The little ones just ignored him, they were too engrossed in the film and this wasn't a rare enough occurrence to interest them.

"Where's my chips?"

"You weren't here," I told him.

Mum got up. "I'll make you some tea," she said.

"Sod your tea. Where's my fish and chips?"

Wearily, I saw mum shake her head. "We didn't know when you were coming in, Tom."

He started calling her all sorts of names and thumping his fist against the wall. He was going on about his being the head of the household and there not being a proper meal ready for him when he got in.

In other circumstances it might even have been funny. He only ever seems to come home when he's drunk. He hasn't had a job since I can remember and mum has kept the house going on the little jobs she manages to get on the side. Head of the household...that was a joke, except no one was laughing.

Everyone in the room was tense waiting to see what he would do next. The little ones edged closer to the TV and tried to pretend they didn't hear. I watched not sure what was coming. I was only aware that I was getting angry when I realised I had clenched my fist around the screwdriver I had been using earlier to unscrew one of Benny's toys to get the batteries in.

As his voice got louder I felt myself rise from the chair, the screwdriver still in my hand.

Mum just stood there.

I suppose years of his tantrums had taught her the best thing was not to do or say anything that might antagonise him. The whole thing was unfair. We had all been having a nice night and in he comes and starts all this.

His voice got rougher and his ranting more incoherent. He went over to the Christmas tree and started on about the toys and things the little ones had left under the tree, about how it was all a waste of money. As if he didn't just drink away all the money he managed to get his hands on.

He picked up Ashley's new doll and threw it across the room. Ashley burst into tears and ran over to rescue it. She ran sobbing into the corner and sat cradling the broken doll, sniffing and wiping her face with her sleeve. Next he started picking up the boys' action figures and little Joey's new car. He threw that across the room and it bounced off the side of the TV and smashed into the fireplace.

I remember watching it disintegrate and spray around the room like chunks of silver hailstones. All the kids were wailing now and that made him worse.

Mum started to say something about upsetting them. He raised his hand to thump mum and something inside me ripped apart letting out all the anger. I am still not sure exactly what made me do it but it had been bubbling up inside me, a volcano of red hot fury, and suddenly I couldn't take it any more.

I pushed mum out of the way and stood up in front of him. Part of me was surprised to find that he was only about an inch taller than me. Although he was almost twice my weight, I was so angry I didn't care. I held the screwdriver inches away from his face and roared at him.

"Just you try and hit Mum again and you'll get this in your face."

There must have been some look in my eye or a note in my voice that got through the drunken haze because he stopped, dead still.

My father actually stopped. Scared of me!

My chest was heaving, growling hot breath forcing itself out of me. It's probably just as well he did stop. At that moment I was someone else, I was like a raging animal, capable of any-thing and I think he recognised it.

I'll never know if I could have gone through with it and stabbed him with the screwdriver because he backed away from me and stomped out of the house. He didn't come back until the next morning.

He's never forgiven me for that but it made me realise I could stand up to him. He only tried to hit mum once more when I was there. When I saw him lift his arm I picked up a chair, trying to get it between him and her. It was fairly solid and he brought his arm down hard. I can still hear the sickening crunch as it broke the bone. It makes me shudder even now, but he's never tried to hit mum again, at least not while I've been in the house.

Davey Hilton is there waiting when I get back from x-ray. Dad turns up but he ignores both of us. He's got his newspaper out and is checking the racing results. A doctor comes in and Hilton listens as she explains that they have checked my foot and also my hip because I had been complaining of a pain there, but there are no broken bones. They are going to keep me in overnight because I have this headache. The pain has mostly gone now but they want to make sure there aren't any problems.

Hilton tells Dad that he needs to come and get me tomorrow. Dad just grunts something about it all being a waste of his time coming in. He gets up, folds his newspaper, sticking it longways into his jacket pocket and goes off without saying a thing to me. Hilton just shakes his head and says he's got the statement. So that's all he needs tonight. He says he'll come in tomorrow morning and see me before I go home.

As he leaves a nurse comes and asks if I want a cup of tea while I wait to go up to the ward. Everyone here is so nice. I've never had so many folk fussing over me in my life. I could get used to this!

I lie back still trying to get my head sorted about Andy.

He isn't dead. It is more than just a relief; I don't know how I could have lived with the thought of having killed him. Andy has always looked up to me and he usually follows along with anything I say. I kind of like it, I suppose. But now I feel as though I've let him down. It's worse because although I can't admit it to anyone, I'm a bit worried about going to see Andy after what Hilton said about the state he's in. All I can imagine in my head is the bloody mess where his face should have been.

What will he look like now?

CHAPTER NINE

Hilton looked at the statement he had taken from Spider, which had not been particularly easy with constant interruptions from his father. None of these had been constructive, mostly along the lines of how stupid the boy was and what he was going to do to the boy to 'sort him out'.

Not for the first time it occurred to him that in different circumstances Spider could have turned out a really nice kid if he had been given half a chance.

His next stop was the High Dependency Ward where he wanted to see if he could meet up with the girl's parents.

As he stood waiting for the lift he watched a couple come into the hospital and approach the reception desk. The receptionist pointed to the lift. They were both tall. The husband was dressed in an immaculate and, as far as Hilton could tell, very expensive suit and his wife, despite the fact it was the middle of the night, was dressed elegantly with that look some women manage, as if she had just stepped out of a beauty parlour. They were making their way to the lift and Hilton guessed that they might be the girl's parents. The man had the same striking dark hair and eyes as his daughter.

They waited behind him; the slightly strained look in their eyes when he nodded at them was the only evidence of their concern.

The lift doors slid open and the couple followed him in.

"Which floor?" he inquired.

"The High Dependency ward," the woman said, her voice wavering slightly. "4th or 5th floor, I'm not sure."

"It's the fourth floor," Hilton told her. He pressed the button and watched the doors glide silently closed. The lift was filled with her expensive perfume.

There was that kind of silence you only get when standing in lifts with strangers. Hilton wondered whether to say something, then decided that he might as well, he would be speaking to them soon enough anyway. He coughed self-consciously. "Do you mind if I ask if it was your daughter who was in the car crash tonight?"

The man stared at him accusingly, as if he had said something obscene, intruded on a private matter, but his wife nodded.

"PC Hilton, Youth Liaison officer. I have been assigned to the case." He held out his hand to the man who shook it firmly, his eyes reassessing Hilton in light of this information.

"I am Mr Shiarto and this is my wife."

"Do you know what happened?" the woman asked. She looked as if she almost didn't want to know. "We've only been told she was hurt in an accident and is unconscious, but that is all they would say."

"I am just trying to get statements myself. The car she was in was stolen and when they crashed your daughter and another boy were hurt. The driver was injured, too."

"A stolen car?" Deanna's mother looked horrified but her father seemed less surprised. His jaw clenched and a look of anger flashed across his eyes, quickly replaced by a guarded expression. Hilton realised he was a man who liked to keep his feelings under strict control.

They were still digesting the information when the lift door opened and they stepped out into the corridor. Hilton followed behind them. The High Dependency ward had an air of calm efficiency, hushed except for the continual subdued bleeping and ticking of monitoring equipment.

Hilton stopped, as they were about to pass through the door. He had decided to find Andy and his family first, to give Deanna's parents a bit of time on their own.

"If you wouldn't mind I would like to have a word with you before you leave the hospital?"

Mr Shiarto nodded. "Very well, Constable." The man turned and followed his wife as a nurse led them away into the ward.

Hilton pressed the lift button to go back down again. He found himself almost reluctant to find Andy's parents. He already knew them because he had been involved in the aftermath of their daughter's death. This was going to be hard for them.

He had a bit of a soft spot for the kid, too. One of the things about living in a relatively small town was that he knew most of the kids quite well. He had known Andy and Spider since they started at high school and while Spider had definitely been the leader, Andy was the clown, always fooling about and never really getting into too much trouble until the last couple of years.

From what the hospital had told him on his first short briefing, Andy was going to need quite a lot of plastic surgery to repair his shattered face, never mind his other injuries.

He passed the waiting room. It was never empty on a Friday night when all the dregs of society seemed to congregate in A&E. He scanned the room. There were two or three drunks, familiar faces, and some wild partygoers whose night out had suddenly turned into a nightmare of blood, broken bones and bruising. A teenage girl with a sparkly top and strange head-gear – fluffy green alien antennae – was wiping her smudged mascara across her tearful face; an anxious middle-aged man with an overcoat hastily donned over pyjamas sat beside a thickset man with purple and black swollen eyes.

Hilton went to reception and inquired where Andy was now. He followed the blue line painted on the floor, as directed, stopping briefly at the kiosk to buy a drink. At least it was hot and wet, which was its only resemblance to coffee.

Tossing the empty cup into a bin he approached a cubicle where Andy's parents were sitting beside an empty bed. They looked small and defeated, as if the weight of the last couple of years had taken all their strength and this latest crisis was more than they could bear.

"Mr & Mrs Macintosh?"

Andy's mum stood up and came towards Hilton.

"PC Hilton, isn't it?" She smiled and her face came alive.

"Good of you to remember me." Hilton was surprised. "How is Andy?"

"He's been taken off for some tests. They asked us to wait here."

"Was he able to tell you anything about what happened?"

"I'm afraid he couldn't say much at all. His jaw is damaged and his face..." Mr Macintosh paused to take a deep breath. "They said he should be able to speak a little, after the operation. The plastic surgeon is with him now. They are going to operate as soon as they can."

"I'm so sorry." Hilton struggled to find anything to say. He stayed and spoke to them for a few minutes and then left with a promise to look in on Andy later.

In a side room off the High Dependency ward the young doctor looked as though she was searching for the right words. Deanna's parents sat like statues waiting to hear the bad news they dreaded, that their precious daughter might not survive, that she might be permanently disabled, that they would never have their bright, smiling, beautiful daughter back again.

"Deanna has a serious concussion but we think there is every possibility that she will recover completely from that and apart from a lot of bruising she has no other major injuries." The doctor gave a re-assuring smile and Deanna's father relaxed his stiff pose, sinking back into the chair as he tried to process the good news.

Deanna's mother narrowed her eyes. "That's not everything, is it?" she asked.

The doctor shook her head and took a moment or two before she replied.

Deanna's father sat up straight, tense again. "What do you mean? You said she should recover completely!"

"We do expect her to recover, Mr Shiarto, it's just that..." the doctor hesitated. "You did know that Deanna was pregnant?"

The doctor watched as the man's face drained of all colour.

"Pregnant?"

He breathed the word as though it had suddenly become difficult to understand. "Are you sure? No, I'm sorry, I know you must be sure or you wouldn't have said anything." He was still searching her face, hoping that he had misunderstood, that it could perhaps be a mistake. "But she's only just 15. That little bastard, I'll kill him!"

"I'm afraid that as a result of the accident she has lost the baby," the doctor said quietly.

Both parents looked stunned, unsure how to react.

The doctor stood up. "I will leave you a few moments in private. The ward sister will let you in to see Deanna when you are ready."

CHAPTER TEN

Andy

Ohmigod, Ohmigod, Ohmigod…I don't know how to handle this. Ohmigod.

"You are going to need quite a bit of fixing up, son," the plastic surgeon had said.

The **PLASTIC** surgeon.

That has always sounded strange to me. Why call it a **plastic** surgeon? It makes you think of all those people who make masks and things for movies, to make people look like they are aliens or give them someone else's face.

Face…My face. What if they get it all wrong and I look like someone else? I kind of liked my face the way it was. Never really thought about it before but it was mine and no one else's.

It was me.

It wasn't the most amazing face in the world but it was the one I expected to see in the mirror in the mornings.

Plastic surgeon. Would he remould my face like a bit of plastic? Ohmigod…peeling bits…no! It can't be like that.

He said he was off to see Mum and Dad, to tell them. They'll crack up. I didn't mean to do this. I didn't want to make them all sad again. I wish Fiona was here. I miss her, but that was all my fault, too.

I should never have let Spider do the Parse Run. I knew he was trying to give it all up.

No, it was all because of HER. Deanna was the one who made him go out on a Run again. He listens to everything she says nowadays. She even gets all pathetic and acts like a baby, especially when she wants Spider to do something she wants. If it wasn't for her…

Typical girl, just like Fiona. Always wanting to go and do things, push it all a bit further.

Fiona was like that. Just because she was a couple of minutes older than me she thought she knew it all. She knew that pond wasn't safe, but she went there anyway. It was all her fault, all of it. Things would have been great if we hadn't gone there that day.

Oh, Fiona I'm sorry. It was my fault. I should have been quicker. I should have let you go first; you might still be alive if I had. I should have climbed down to you, but I was too scared. It was my fault, all of it.

"Are you in pain?" the nurse asked. She mopped the tears that had escaped below the bandages and I suddenly felt them stinging on my face.

I hadn't even realised anyone was there.

I shake my head. It's easier than speaking. I don't know if I can speak. Every time I move my face it's like I am pulling and tearing another bit, so I'm trying not to move it at all.

The nurse is chattering on about prepping me for the operation. I try to ignore what she's doing. I don't care what happens to me any more.

"Your parents are going to come in and see you for a moment before you fall asleep."

Fall asleep. I don't feel in the least sleepy. Perhaps that was what that jab was for, well, if it was it didn't work.

Mum and dad look as miserable as I thought they would when they come into the room. To the rest of the world they probably give the impression of being okay but I know that look in their eyes. It has always been there since Fiona died and it always gets worse when I do something to make them worry.

Mum has been crying, a lot. She is trying to be brave but she can hardly bear to look at me. Is my face so bad or is she just angry with me for doing something else to upset them? That seems to be all I do these days so why change now. Why don't they realise that it hurt me too, when Fiona died? She was my twin sister, mine.

Dad is trying to be all jolly but that is almost worse, so false that I cringe for him. He has started telling me not to worry it will all be fine.

Mum looks like she is trying to hold back the tears again. Thankfully the nurse comes in and tells them they can only have a few moments because they are waiting for me in the operating theatre. As they say goodbye mum tells me again not to worry about anything, that they will be waiting and will be there when I wake up.

Now that does get me worrying. It starts me panicking.

What if I start talking about things when I'm coming out of the anaesthetic? Talking about the day Fiona died. They would find out. Everyone would find out. They might decide it was murder and send me to prison.

Ohmigod! I can't let them put me to sleep.

The nurse is saying something about counting to ten. Doing it in my head if I don't want to speak.

Why would I want to do that? I suppose I should do what she wants, there's bound to be some silly reason. Ouch! That hurt. Another jab!

"You can start counting now, Andy."

"One…two…three…"

CHAPTER ELEVEN

Spider

Deanna took me to her house once. Always wondered how people like her lived and what it was like inside their fancy houses high up on Howard Hill. I didn't want to go, well I did really, but I didn't want her parents to catch me there. Deanna says her Dad thinks she is too young to have a boyfriend and I can just imagine his face if he found us there, together.

Her mum works for one of those big corporations who have letters instead of a name. She looks like someone from one of those American soaps, always done up and perfect. I'd hate my mum to look like that. She wouldn't seem real somehow.

My mum is soft and comfy, always at home when you need her and ready to put on the kettle at any moment in the day. It would be nice to see her all done up, apart from going to funerals and things like that. That was the only time I've seen mum all tarted up. When I was 10 we all went to my granddad's funeral and Mum gave me a clout around the ear when I appeared in my football shirt.

"You'll not shame me by going to your granddad's funeral dressed like that."

It was probably the only time I've ever seen dad wear a tie. Not that it did much for him. The tie looked like it was tied too tight and was trying to choke him. The collar of his shirt was all screwed up and his fat beer belly made a joke of his only 'smart' jacket. I think it had been bought when he was still working. Mum was furious with him when he tried it on but she insisted he wear it anyway.

I couldn't imagine Deanna's dad ever looking like that, I've never seen him in anything but a smart suit, except for the pictures Deanna showed me of her on holiday with her parents when they went to Africa on safari. They were all wearing the most amazing clothes that Deanna said they had bought while they were there, all African looking with brilliant colours and patterns, nothing drab or dowdy. Her mum was wearing a sort of turban thing on her head and huge earrings. Deanna was wearing a brightly coloured dress, too, nothing like the clothes she wears the rest of the time but she looked terrific in it. It goes somehow with her dark eyes. If I wore something like that I would look so pale and pathetic.

Their house smelled different, kind of weird and exotic. Deanna said it was the cigars her dad liked to smoke. She laughed and said her mum hated them but she still bought him them for his birthday because she knew how much he enjoyed them. It must be weird to have parents like that, I couldn't make up my mind if I was jealous of it all or not.

There were lots of rooms on the ground floor, all perfect and tidy as though it was a museum. There were carved wooden animals and modern art sculptures all over the place and tall vases with huge leaves in them and no flowers. I was scared I would trip over and break something but I acted cool as though I was in places like that all the time.

The floor was dark glossy polished wood with rugs here and there, not like our house, where the only reason you can see the floorboards is because we had to throw away the carpet because it had so many holes in it that mum kept tripping up on them. We never could afford a new carpet.

I don't think I could ever live somewhere like that, I wouldn't feel comfortable. It was all too perfect, not like a real home, more like something out of a fancy magazine.

We went upstairs to her room. It was enormous and there were clothes scattered all over the place.

"I don't usually let Mrs Benther clean in here, I don't like anyone messing about with my things but every now and then my mum insists and I can't find anything for ages."

"Who's Mrs Benther?"

"The cleaning lady. She usually comes in a few mornings a week and on special days when mum's having a dinner party or something.

Deanna said her parents wouldn't be home for hours so we settled down to listen to some music and after a while it was easy to enjoy being there with her and to forget that we were in her parents' house. Or perhaps that was what made it all the more exciting, the thought of getting caught.

CHAPTER TWELVE

Deanna

Everything was white, just like fresh snow. It was just as bright, too. I was sure I could hear sleigh bells, but they sounded a bit wrong, too regular. I knew I must be dreaming when I saw a baby lying in the snow. It looked happy and content but then as I watched it turned to look at me and I found myself staring at Spider's face.

I tried to reach out to him but the whole world had changed, it was all upside down and Spider looked worried. I tried to tell him it was okay, that it was snowing. I love the freshly fallen snow, just before anyone has put their footprints in it. I wanted Spider to come and mess about in the snow with me, but he disappeared.

I reached out but for some reason I couldn't move my hand and the snow had all vanished. I called to Spider but he had gone, too.

For a while I was wandering about the streets in the rain until I realized I was looking for something. It worried me that I couldn't find it. It was my responsibility. I knew this was something I had to do by myself, no one else could do it, I had to find it and make sure it was safe but I wasn't sure exactly what it was I was looking for.

Then I remembered.

My father appeared. Dad and I have always been close but I knew he wouldn't understand. I was trying to pretend everything was fine and we had this crazy conversation and all the time I was worrying about how I could get away to go and look for the baby.

Next thing I knew we were in a car. I felt safe because Spider was there, but he wasn't happy. He was driving quite slowly and I wanted him to speed up. I told him I'd never find the baby if he drove so slowly but he just smiled at me and ignored what I said as if he hadn't heard me at all.

The bells were still ringing only now it seemed much more like they were buzzing and bleeping. I could hear my mother's voice telling me it would be all right. She sounded sad. I wanted to tell her something important but I couldn't remember what it was.

Mum's voice faded away and I was back wandering through the Parse. I don't really like going down to the Parse unless Spider is with me. It is full of drunks and pushers, 'wasters' as Dad calls them. I thought I could hear Dad's voice but then it all faded away again.

It hurts when I move and my eyelids feel so heavy that I can't be bothered to open my eyes.

Dad still calls me his little baby but he can't see I've grown up now and can think for myself so he is always trying to protect me. He says that Spider comes from a bad family and is no good for me but he just doesn't understand. When he saw Spider and me together he nearly hit the roof, and we were only kissing.

He and mum can't seem to understand that I want to be with Spider. I love him. He makes me feel so special and he takes care of me and lets me be myself, not the perfect little daughter that they want me to be.

If they had their way I would be this studious, tidy, good little girl that had no fun, stayed home every night and listened to bedtime stories with my mum and dad as if I was ten, with absolutely no personality at all, just a clone of mum.

So what if I want to have a stud on my tongue or a ring in my belly button? It's not the end of the world.

I'm so very tired. I can't remember what that important thing was. I think it had something to do with Spider. Spider is probably away with Andy just now. They are always together. I don't think Andy likes me much. He puts up with me because otherwise Spider gets angry, but I can see it in his eyes when he thinks Spider isn't looking. Andy wants me to just disappear so that he and Spider can be together as they used to be.

The baby.

That's what I was trying to remember.

I think it was when I missed for the second month running that I realized something was definitely wrong. Before that I had tried to convince myself that I was being melodramatic. Pregnant...? Ha. Not me! Never! I wouldn't be that stupid. That was what happened to other girls - the stupid ones. I knew better, it couldn't possibly have happened to me.

I suppose that deep down, where you can't hide even from yourself, I probably knew. I kept on remembering that day, running it through my mind like a favourite film. Spider and me, together.

I wanted to do it as much as he did. It sort of felt right, inevitable. Afterwards I felt as if everyone would be able to tell, just by looking at me, that I was different somehow.

I knew my dad would kill Spider if he ever found out. He has this idea that I am this little princess, like a china doll on a shelf, virginal and untouchable. I love my dad but he has absolutely no idea who I am and he wouldn't understand if I told him.

I want to be an actress and I'm quite good at acting, too. Dad just says that it's all right for fun but I have to study and work hard to get a profession. He is sure that I am going to become a doctor or a vet or - God forbid - a dentist, like him! Some chance.

Spider helps me feel more like myself, like I want to be.

I felt like I had a glorious secret, all especially mine. It was even more special because Spider didn't change afterwards, like as if he had got what he wanted and then didn't respect me anymore, the way they tell it in all the soaps and the girls who write in to all those agony aunts in magazines.

He still wanted to see me, to be with me just as much as I wanted to be with him.

I suppose I wasn't really all that sure of him. That's why I didn't tell him about the baby. I wasn't sure he would want to know. He loves the idea that I can wear all my skimpy tops and fancy clothes, he's always telling me that, so how would he react if I told him I was pregnant and was going to get all fat and lumpy looking? He'd probably run a mile.

It's not as if I have any other friends I can talk to about it either. All the goody, studious types turned their backs on me when I started going out with Spider and found out I had better things to do, rather than studying. They made faces behind my back and made loud comments that Spider was rough and common, and how could I bear to let him touch me? They were really nasty.

Not that I bothered about them but sometimes I miss the girly things. I'm usually too busy with Spider to notice but it would have been quite nice to have a friend to talk to about it, before I tell Spider.

But I don't really need them anyway.

I went out and bought a pregnancy test. I still couldn't believe it when I saw it turn blue, so I went to two other chemists in town and bought one from each of them but they all said the same.

I locked myself away in my room trying to understand what was happening to me. I still couldn't believe it. I must have sat there for hours, luckily mum wasn't home because she had some conference or other to go to. Just as well, I had no idea what I was going to do.

Eventually I decided I wouldn't do anything. I suppose part of me hoped that if I ignored it, it would just disappear. I didn't want to tell Spider yet anyway, that would have made it all too real. While no one else knew I could pretend it wasn't happening at all.

CHAPTER THIRTEEN

Spider

There is no way I am going to get to sleep. The bed is like sleeping on the floor only not as comfortable, and there are folk coming and going even though it's late into the night. I think I must be in the old folk's ward, it is full of moans and groans and nurses who don't seem to understand the concept of quiet. Every time I move every bit of my body screams as though a truck has driven over me.

I suppose I must have drifted off now and then because now it's morning and the noise has started again for real.

I thought hospitals were quiet places but from six o'clock in the morning everyone starts crashing and bashing about, opening cupboards and bringing round trolleys with watery tea. Why anyone in their right mind would want a cup of tea at that time of the morning, I have no idea.

The woman who brings the tea round is a bit like my granny used to be and she doesn't seem to bother that I don't want to speak to her. I don't want to speak to anyone. She chatters on to all the patients whether anyone answers her or not.

All through the night I had been running through what had happened, why it happened and how my life got to this shitty place.

Hilton said he was pretty sure I am going to be sent away this time and he's probably right. It's not that it bothers me for myself, might be okay really, but how will mum get by with the old man coming back in totally pissed and trying to beat her up all the time. For the last few months I've been staying in until he staggered back home, not going out to meet up with the gang until I knew he had passed out in the chair, which never took very long. But at least he didn't take things out on mum when I was there. But if I'm away I know he'll think there's nothing to stop him.

Shit!

Then there's Deanna. Hilton said she was still unconscious, when he dropped in to see me last night before he left. That was when he dropped the bombshell that kept me tossing about all night.

Pregnant? That really did my head in! It was only that one time.

I would have been a father. I turn the word around in my mind; whisper it to see how it sounds.

I quickly look about to make sure no one has seen or heard me. It makes things look different for some reason, probably because of my dad. I would never be like him. But I'm not going to be a father anyway because Deanna has lost the baby and I'm the one to blame.

I really am a murderer.

I can't think about that just now, so many things are crowding into my head. But every time I try to think of something else it pushes its way back in.

A murderer. I murdered my own baby.

The nurse comes by and asks if I want some breakfast but the thought of it makes me want to puke. I shake my head but then she starts pestering me to take something so in the end I give in, just to shut her up. I need time to think and I know that my stomach is churning so much that if I ate anything it would just end up spewed back up again, so what is the point?

Andy. I can think about Andy.

Not sure that is any better, though. When I thought he was dead and found out he wasn't, I had been so happy to find out he was still alive. But last night I asked the nurse if he could find out how Andy was. He came back later to say Andy was in the operating theatre getting some plastic surgery done on his face. It sounds nasty.

How could I have been so stupid? I hadn't been going to do the Run ever again. I told myself that I was going to stop all that so that I could start one of these courses on mechanics that Hilton had told me about and then get a job and make some money.

I wish I'd never gone near that car.

Hilton said I would be going home today, they were only keeping me in overnight to make sure the dizzy spell and headache I had wasn't anything serious. He said he would come round and see me when he comes in.

Dad has to come and collect me. Hilton said, I am supposed to be in my parent's custody so I have to wait for my old man to come and get me. Could be a long wait, knowing him. My social worker is supposed to be coming in, too.

Brilliant. She's such a pain in the butt!

She is always trying too hard to make me think she understands me and that she can help. Not a chance! She hasn't got a clue.

Anyway, I have to hang around here until the doctors have

done their rounds and then I want to go and see Andy and Deanna. They'd better not try to stop me.

After the doctors came on their ward round they told me I can get dressed but I have to wait for my Dad before I leave the ward.

My foot is beginning to ache. They wrapped it up in a stretchy bandage last night but the nurse tells me I might be able to get my trainers over it, if I leave the laces undone. I can walk on it, just, but she says I am to try to stay off it for a few days. Not likely, there's no way I'm going to sit about at home.

"Hello, Spider."

I groan inwardly.

She has arrived, Mary, my social worker; the answer to all the world's problems – or so she thinks. I hope she won't stay long, but I know her better than that.

"How are you feeling? You look like you've been in the wars. Those are some bruises you've got."

I mumble something, not even sure what, but it seems to satisfy her. I really can't be bothered speaking to her but I know from past experience that she will hang around and pester me until I tell her enough to satisfy her curiosity.

"So, would you like to tell me what happened? The last time we spoke you said you weren't going to steal cars any more. We talked about what that would mean for you, didn't we?"

She is wearing her 'I am disappointed in you' face. I know it well.

I turn away and look out of the window. I can't be bothered with all this right now.

"Just trying to show off to your girlfriend, were you? Trying to show her how clever you are?"

I know she is goading me trying to make me speak to her, to get me to tell her what happened. I don't want to speak to her but all the unfairness of it boils up so much that I can't stop myself.

"It wasn't like that. She wanted to do it. She wanted to see what it was like. It was just going to be that one time, then I was going to stop."

I can see she doesn't believe me.

"I was! Really I was! Nobody will believe that, now. Will they?"

She shrugs. "You've said it before, Spider."

"But this time I was." I shake my head. "No one ever believes me, anyway."

"So what exactly happened?"

I try to remember what had started the whole thing off. It had probably been during the day when Deanna and I had been walking down the street, talking about cars, the Parse Run and what it felt like. She had been so excited by the whole thing and wanted to see what it was like.

"I'd love to go on a Run," Deanna gave me that smile she uses whenever she is trying to get me to agree to something. It is always difficult to say, no, when she does that.

"Girls don't usually go on Runs."

I shrugged. I suppose I realised I'd said the wrong thing the moment I'd said it. Saying anything like that to Deanna is like setting a match to a car, you stood well back and hoped the blaze didn't burn you.

"Really?" she said, dangerously.

I cringed inside, waiting for the explosion. It wasn't long in coming.

"Why not? Do you think girls aren't up for it? Not able to take the pressure? Not able to drive fast or something?"

I held up my hands to ward off the slagging I was about to get. "I give up. It's just that usually....Usually, girls don't do it, they don't usually want to."

"Well, this girl does. Or don't you think I can hack it?"

I denied that one quickly. There was very little that Deanna wouldn't do if she wanted to.

That was when Andy came across the road towards us.

"Hi, Spider, what're you doing?"

"Spider tells me girls don't go on Runs," Deanna told him scornfully.

"They don't," Andy shrugged. "I've never known a girl to go on a Run, ever."

"There's always a first time." Deanna was not about to let this go. "What about tonight?"

"I dunno." Andy scuffed his feet at the wall beside us. He was waiting for me to tell her, no; that she couldn't go. I could see it in his eyes.

"Spider?" Deanna said, coaxingly. She leaned against me and looked straight into my eyes. I was hooked.

"I suppose. What do you think, Andy? We could do one tonight? Just a quick Run, no probs."

In the end Andy was always keen. He loved the speed and the excitement of it all and he hadn't been too delighted when I had told him I wasn't doing it any more. He said he understood why and all that. I could see he really wasn't happy about Deanna going along. In the end who cared who was there? The Run was the thing.

After it got dark we met up and headed off to one of the housing estates. Joe and Baz had tagged along as soon as they heard there was a Run going on. They're a pain but they're friends of Andy's.

I had seen a really hot car, a black BMW, that hadn't moved for a week or so. It was just old enough that I could get into it without too much trouble. The street was quite dark and a light misty rain made the streetlights cast an eerie glow as we came down the road. It was ideal weather, no moon and damp enough to keep folks at home.

I showed them the car and we all walked past it along the street to the end, to make sure no one was around, watching. I could feel the usual buzz, the anticipation, the fear, the excitement. This time there was a surge of pride. I knew how to do this and I could show Deanna just how good I was.

As we walked back to the car I got Joe and Baz to keep watch on the street. Deanna watched me break into the car. I learnt the trick from one of the older boys who had let me come along on my first Run, and then I had added my own flair to it. I could get into most cars, easily and quietly; I was good at it.

With the doors open they all piled in. Andy climbed into the front to give me a hand breaking the steering lock and he was about to slide across into the passenger seat as usual, when I stopped him.

"It's her first Run, Andy, Deanna should sit up front."

Andy made a face.

"It was her idea," I insisted. "C'mon, Andy, we can't hang

about." I glanced along the street. It was important to move as quickly as you could once you got into the car. It was just plain stupid to get caught at this stage.

Andy wasn't pleased but he jumped into the back with Joe and Baz. I started the car and gunned the engine. We were off.

CHAPTER FOURTEEN

Andy

Fiona used to swing her hair when she walked. I liked watching it, the way all the separate blonde strands fanned out and then fell neatly into place again.

It wasn't all fanned out when they brought her out of the water; it was hanging in thick clumps, wet and dark. There were stringy bits of weeds clinging to the back of her head. They looked slimy and greasy. I remember thinking Fiona would have hated that, she was so finicky about her hair.

I can still hear her voice when she came bursting into my room that morning.

"Get up, lazy. It's the most stupendously, gorgeous morning."

"Go away!" I grumbled and pulled the covers over my head.

"Aw, Come on!" Fiona would never give up when she had something in her head. "It's a really hard frost. The pond will be frozen over. We can make a slide again, just like last year."

She grabbed a handful of my bed covers and tugged them off onto the floor. I had a squint at my alarm clock. It was only eight o'clock. Fiona had this thing about getting up early at weekends.

"It's cold, Fiona, leave me alone!"

I tried to get the covers back but she just laughed and ran out of the room pulling them behind her.

"Fiona, come back!"

It was hopeless. I knew I would just have to get up. Part of me wanted to anyway. The pond only froze over for about a week each year and it was usually a race to see who could get there first to make the best slide, but I knew that wasn't the only reason Fiona was so desperate to get there.

All along the far side of the pond is a wall of rock and in the middle is an overhang, a sharp finger of stone that juts out.

It's called the Hook.

All the rest of the year the only way to climb out onto the Hook is by going around the long way, and coming at it from the top. In winter, when the pond is frozen over, you can walk right underneath the Hook where there are hand and foot holds so that you can climb it.

It's a difficult climb and last year Fiona tried twice but she just couldn't get to the top. She was even more furious that she didn't make it and I did. I knew she had been waiting for the first hard frost to try again.

I grabbed something to wear from the pile on the floor and then spent another few minutes searching for one of my gloves.

By this time Fiona was ready almost jumping about

in frustration. "Come on, Andy. Everyone else will get there first if you don't get a move on."

I found the glove, stuck behind my computer and held it up with a grin. "Got it!"

The streets were pretty quiet as we raced down through the lane, ducking under the overgrown trees and branches that threatened to crown us with their thick layer of snow. On across the road, past the shops, Fiona was taking exaggerated jumping steps, leaving giant footprints in the thick snow covering the grass of the football fields. Her white jacket matched the snow and I told her if she stayed still someone might mistake her for a snowman. She stopped like a statue with her hands on her hips and sang a few bars of Frosty the Snowman before racing on ahead of me again.

I caught sight of Joe on his paper round. He waved at us and I veered off to see him. Fiona skidded to a halt and cut across the grass to follow me.

We stood talking to Joe for a bit but Fiona was getting agitated.

"Come on, Andy," she moaned.

Joe was telling me about the new computer game he had been playing the night before and eventually Fiona got really cheesed off and started walking away.

"I'm off down to the pond," she said. "I'm not waiting."

Joe looked at his watch and said he had to go anyway or he'd be in trouble with the paper shop for not getting the papers delivered on time. I ran off after Fiona and we both headed towards the pond.

The pond was deserted and the Hook loomed over the far side, dark and threatening. There were pockets of snow in the crevices. It was going to be a hard, cold climb.

We walked cautiously across the snow-covered ice. It felt solid under our feet but I stamped hard a few times before I went right onto it; to make sure there was no chance of it cracking. Fresh snow was falling, drifting through the air as though it wasn't heavy enough to fall straight down. Everything looked fresh and crisp.

When we got to the foot of the Hook it towered over us, huge and forbidding. The overhang stands three times as tall as me, and leans over the pond making a shadowy shelter. I had climbed it last year but I had forgotten how hard a climb it had been. Standing underneath it I rubbed my hands together to get them warmed up.

"I'll go first," I told her.

I thought she was about to argue but she just nodded.

The first part is easy because there are lots of hand and foot holds. It gets more difficult as you go up. Once you are past the overhang of the Hook it becomes large flat slabs of black rock, slippy with fresh snow and scarily high above the pond.

I got past the first easy bit and stopped to rub some feeling back into my frozen fingers. Fiona was right behind me, just about under my feet.

"Come on, Andy!"

"Give me a minute, my hands are freezing."

I started climbing again and was halfway up when I turned to look down at Fiona. This was where she had given up last year.

"Are you okay?"

"I'm fine!" She kept on climbing, getting closer to my feet. She sounded a bit peeved that I had asked her at all. "Just keep on going," she grunted. "Don't stop."

"Okay."

I climbed another step higher, and then another. The snow was still falling. My boots slipped as I reached for a handhold. I scrabbled around to get a grip, sending some shale showering down on top of Fiona who was now right underneath me. She yelled at me to watch what I was doing. I moved my foot carefully and found another foothold, wider than before. I shook my hand and flexed my frozen fingers. Reaching up for the next crevice in the rock, I pulled myself up.

That was when it happened.

It all happened quickly at the time but I've relived it so often in nightmares in slow motion.

I move my foot; my hands are frozen and aching even through my gloves. My other foot slips from the narrow ridge of rock and swings through the air. Hanging on by my hands I feel them beginning to slip. I scrabble at the rock face with my feet trying to find a crevice, anything, to take the weight from my slipping fingers. I find a toehold with one foot and as I'm kicking out to try and get the other foot higher my foot hits something soft.

Fiona cries out. I turn and watch her claw at the rock face. She looks up at me in surprised horror as she slips down under the Hook. Her scream, a long shriek, resounds across the frozen pond. I hear a sickening crack as she hits the ice.

I stare down below me to where she had been climbing a moment before. The overhang hides her from view and I can't move. I'm screaming her name- but I can't move. I know I should be climbing down or up. Doing something to get to her – but I can't move.

I can't move.

A large black bird flies past me, the only moving living thing in the snow-covered landscape.

I yell her name, but Fiona doesn't answer. I yell again but it just echoes in the air and then silence. I force myself to do something and I start to move my hand.

I'm climbing up.

Part of me wants to climb back down but I'm almost at the top. I deny the small voice that's telling me I don't want to go down because of what I might find there. I tell myself it will be quicker this way.

Something inside tells me it won't make any difference. Folk say that twins have some kind of bond; they know what is happening to the other one. I don't ever remember it being so strong before that day. Inside I know but I don't really believe it, I don't want to, I can't.

I keep telling myself that Fiona is just winding me up, that she's down there hiding from me and laughing at me.

Eventually I scramble up onto the top of the rock. I lie flat over the snowy ledge and try to see her but I can't see past the Hook at all. Scrambling to my feet I run down the hill behind it, the chill air biting at my throat as I gasp for breath.

I feel like I've been running forever. The path down the hill and around to the pond seems longer than I ever remember. I'm running fast, I've always been a good runner but it feels like I'm hardly moving. I can't go any faster, my chest is burning, seared by the cold air that heaves into my lungs, but I ignore it. My legs are trembling and threatening to collapse under me, but it doesn't matter; nothing matters, I just have to get back there, back to Fiona.

The trail seems never-ending as I race down, slithering and stumbling over frozen tree twigs and branches until I reach flat ground but now I'm at the other side of the hill. It's slippery with snow but I've never run so fast in my life. I slip and slide as I tear along the path all the way back to the pond.

I'm almost there.

When I get to the pond there's still no one else around. It looks smooth and untouched, as though no one has ever been there at all. As if it hasn't happened.

For a moment I almost believe I've imagined it.

I call out to Fiona. Why doesn't she answer? Why is she still messing about? My voice cracks and quivers but it gets stronger as I take a breath and shout again and again, but there is only the silence, filled with the eerie rustle of the soft breeze.

I've never felt so alone.

CHAPTER FIFTEEN

Deanna

"She should never have been allowed so much freedom." Dad's voice is quiet but he sounds angry underneath.

Mum stands up for me. "She's growing up and needs a bit of freedom."

"Look where it's got her, Mel!"

I can almost hear Dad clenching his teeth. He does that when he is angry or worried. "Pregnant! She's only fifteen! It must have been that boy. What's his name? That rough kid who is always hanging around her?"

"Spider," Mum whispers, almost beneath her breath. "I told her not to see him any more, but you know how determined she can be."

It's strange to hear them talking about me as if I'm not there. I think about opening my eyes and telling them I'm listening but it seems to be far too difficult. I'm so very tired.

"I could strangle him. I can't bear to think of him with her. She's only a baby herself, for heaven's sake! She's underage. I'll make sure he goes away for a long time for this. He could have killed her." Dad sounds furious. I wouldn't like him to meet up with Spider when he's so angry.

"We have to realise that she is not a child anymore. I don't think she's quite so easily led into things she doesn't want to do."

I'm surprised to hear Mum saying something like that, she is always on my back when I want to go out, or get home late.

They don't say anything for a while and I drift off to sleep again. I know I should try and open my eyes but I don't feel up to dealing with dad in the state he's in. I'm not ready for an argument.

I can hear the bleeping of a machine close to my head when I wake up again. Mum is somewhere in the room speaking to someone. She's too far away for me to hear properly. I still have my eyes closed but I know it's mum. I realise that I can hear her if I concentrate.

"...she will be able to have children, when she's older, won't she?"

The other voice is lower and I can't quite make it out. It's a strange thing for Mum to be asking. It's difficult to think about looking after one baby far less others. Mum's taking the whole pregnancy thing very well. I thought she would have been just as angry as Dad.

"It was probably for the best," mum's saying. "She's far too young. I just worry about how she will take it when she finds out she's lost the baby."

Lost the baby? My baby? Perhaps this is just another bad dream, a nightmare.

I struggle to fight through the layers of sleep-
iness and force my mouth to work. All that
comes out is a croak but it brings mum and the
doctor rushing to the bed. I can't seem to get
my eyes to stay open for more than a moment
at a time, but I have to find out. I have to ask.

"Deanna!" Mum has tears in her eyes. "It's
going to be all right, darling. You're fine now,
you're safe."

I am so tired and my head is aching but I have
to ask her. All the time when I didn't want to
think that I might be pregnant it was different.
Now that something might have happened to
my precious baby I realise how much I want it.
This is my baby, Spider's and mine.

"Mum, the baby?"

My voice comes out all croaky and I'm not
sure she has understood me. She says nothing
for a moment or two then she nods gently.

"I know all about it, darling. But everything's
going to be all right. You don't have to worry
about anything."

I am tempted to drift off into the secure feeling that everything will be sorted now that
mum is here and she knows about the baby, but
a doubt keeps nagging at me. Had I dreamt it?

"But is the baby…Is it all right?"

I hold my breath waiting for her to answer but
I know deep down that I hadn't been dreaming
when I see the look in her eyes. She bites on
the side of her lip and starts stroking my hand.

"It happened in the car crash. You've been unconscious. There was nothing anyone could have done."

"My baby." I wail. I feel a hard sharp pain in my throat as if I've swallowed a jagged lump of broken glass.

I killed my baby.

I don't know how to stop the tears. What will he say? Then I remember that I haven't told Spider yet. I was so afraid that he would be scared off and stop seeing me. Part of me wants to believe that he would never do that but I've never been completely sure. Now I just want to disappear back down into the nothingness and never wake up. Anywhere that will stop the hurt. I just want to see Spider. He'll make it all right.

"Where's Spider?"

I can't make out the look that passes across Mum's face when she hears me ask.

"I want to see Spider, Mum. Where is he? Is he all right?"

Had Spider been killed in the crash?

"Is he all right?" I ask again, my eyes searching for the answer in her face. I stop breathing for a moment, terrified of her answer but desperate to hear it.

"He's fine, Deanna, but I don't think you should worry about him just now. Just concentrate on getting better yourself. Dad will have a fit if he hears you asking to see Spider after all this.

Just concentrate on getting better."

I grab her hand hard. "He is all right, isn't he? You're not just saying that?"

"No, he is the least hurt of all of you. Now, no more about him and that's the end of that. You need to rest."

CHAPTER SIXTEEN

Spider

I shrug on my denim jacket. I am ready to be discharged from the hospital but I have to wait for my father to come to take me home. They insisted that I couldn't go home on my own, something to do with legal responsibility, which as far as I see means someone who is responsible. Why they think my old man is responsible for anyone when he's usually so pissed he can't even find his own way home most days. There are times I wish he wouldn't come home at all.

Waiting for my father is a pretty hopeless occupation. I know I'll be waiting all day until he gets kicked out of the pub.

I spoke to mum on the phone this morning but she was so upset that I came off the phone as quickly as I could. I don't really care how long it takes, waiting for Dad, I want to go and see Deanna and Andy first, anyway.

I struggle to get my trainer on my foot over the heavy bandage. The only way it works is if I leave all the laces really loose and force my foot into it. It's a bit tight and not very comfortable. One nurse suggested that I could wear some kind of slipper instead but I told him that I wasn't about to go outside with a stupid slipper on my foot, so it was my trainers or nothing.

The nurse in charge of the ward stops me at the door.

"Where are you off to, young man?" I think she has a really sweet smile. "You can't just get up and leave us, you know."

"I want to go and see my friends before my dad comes to get me." I put on my most pathetic wheedling face and I can see it beginning to work on her. "Can you find out what wards they're in?"

She makes a face. "I could. But you will have to promise me you will come back here as soon as you have been to see them. No bunking off and leaving the hospital."

"No prob. I'll come right back," I assure her. "My Dad's not likely to come for me until late this afternoon, anyway. I'll be back for lunch! Never been known to refuse a free meal!"

"Typical boy!" an older nurse laughs as she passes us.

The younger one shakes her head at me and goes off to make a call to find out where Andy and Deanna are. She comes back a few minutes later.

"Deanna is in the High Dependency unit on Ward 6, that's the fourth floor. You could probably get in to see her for a little while, if you're very polite. Your friend, Andy, is in Ward 10 on the sixth floor."

CHAPTER SEVENTEEN

Davey Hilton approached the hospital entrance slow-ly. It was a beautiful morning, bright and fresh and he was reluctant to enter the building knowing that he was likely to be inside for a while. This was the time he missed smoking. It would have given him a rea-son to hang about outside for a bit longer. There was light rain forecast for later in the day and he thought for a moment how much he would rather be enjoying the sunshine sitting quietly fishing by the side of a river. He sighed and stepped in through the hospital doors.

He ran through his list for the day. He had to get a statement from Andy, if he was able to speak, and check up on Deanna and see how she was. The doc-tor had thought she would be conscious by this morn-ing. There was still the matter of the other two who were in the car. Hilton had only found out about them from the paramedic on the scene of the accident.

When he called in about the crash Spider had told the ambulance control about others who had run off and left them but he had been reluctant to say anything about them. Spider would never want to be seen as a 'grass'.

Hilton had a pretty good idea who it had been. He had been dealing with the local kids for so long he knew them all. Who their friends were, where they lived and for some of them, like Spider, he even knew their date of birth.

After checking at reception whether any of his intended interviewees had been moved to other wards, Hilton made his way up in the lift.

On the second floor the lift doors opened and Spider limped in. He stopped short when he saw Hilton.

"Where are you off to, Spider?"

"They said I could go and see Deanna and Andy." Spider pressed the button for the sixth floor. "Just as long as I go back to the ward afterwards."

The metal doors slid closed and the lift started moving smoothly upwards again.

"I'll come down to the ward to see you when I'm finished here," Hilton told him. "When are they letting you go home?"

Spider scowled. "I've to wait until someone comes to get me."

They both knew he would be waiting a long time before his father eventually made it to the hospital. The lift stopped and the doors opened again. Hilton stepped out. He put his hand in to stop the doors from closing.

"If your dad's not arrived by the time I'm through, do you want me to give you a lift home?"

"Yeah."

The kid looked terrible, not just the multi-coloured bruises that had blossomed during the night on his cheeks and jaw, but his eyes looked dark and defeated. This was a side of Spider that Hilton had never seen before. "It'll take me a while yet, though. I've a few statements to get."

"I'll wait down in the ward," Spider managed a slight smile. "They promised me lunch before I go."

"Okay, Spider. I'll come down when I've finished." Hilton let go of the door. As it slid closed a large hand jammed in the doorway, forcing the doors to open again.

"Spider?" a deep voice growled.

Hilton spun around to see who it was. Two inches from his face was Deanna's father.

"That's him, isn't it?" The man snarled at Hilton across the inches that separated them, his face flushed. "He's the useless little sod who was driving the car; isn't he? I'll break his neck."

Hilton turned to see Spider shrinking back against the back wall of the lift. Deanna's father was still holding the door open and appeared to be waiting for a response.

Hilton stared down Deanna's father and placed a firm hand on the man's arm compelling him to remove his hand and allow the door to slide closed.

"I don't think this is going to help matters, Mr Shiarto. I was just on my way to have a word with you. Shall we go back into the ward?"

Deanna's father stood for a moment glowering at Hilton before turning and heading off down the corridor. Hilton checked to make sure Spider had taken the opportunity to escape. Above the lift doors the counter was registering an upper floor.

❖ ❖ ❖

When he eventually left Deanna's ward Hilton wondered what would have happened if he had not managed to persuade her father that going after Spider was not a good idea. He was a powerful bloke and he looked as if he was ready to give Spider a real thumping. Hilton recalled him saying last night that he wanted to make an example of Spider, that he never wanted him free to do this to anyone else's daughter.

Deanna's mother was a calming influence on him but Hilton was happier when Mr Shiarto left saying he had work to do. It would hopefully keep him out of the hospital until Spider had gone home.

Hilton remembered the look he had seen in Spider's eyes. He knew that nothing the courts or anyone else did to Spider would be worse than what he was doing to himself. Basically he was a good kid, or he could have been if he'd had half Deanna's chances.

How screwed up was life?

There were some really bad kids, the kind you almost hoped would never survive the mayhem they caused, but they usually did. Then there were others, like Andy, whose whole life gets turned inside out when he loses his sister and is unable to do anything about it. How could anyone, far less a 12 year old, go on after that?

Deanna on the other hand had a completely different life. She was bright. She had caring wealthy parents whose only fault might have been that they were career minded and worked long hours. They were so determined to give their only daughter all the good things in life when they might have been better spending a bit more time with her, instead.

The situation itself might have given her some problems, but then Spider had come along. She had been looking for a way to break out and he had been the route she'd chosen.

Born into trouble Spider had known little else all his life. But there had been others who had come from the same kind of background and managed to deal with it.

As Hilton made his way towards the lift he unwrapped a bar of chocolate. It was the only thing that helped him get thought the day without a cigarette, but it wasn't doing his thickening waistline any good. He wanted to get hold of Spider and talk to him. He thought he could get through to the boy.

CHAPTER EIGHTEEN

Andy

Spider came in to see me today. He looked pretty rough, not just the bruises but he had this look in his eyes as if he was stunned. He kept on apologising for crashing the car and he wouldn't listen when I told him it was okay. I must look a pretty awful sight so I tried to make a joke of things but he wouldn't lighten up at all.

Then he told me about Deanna, and her having been pregnant. I didn't think he had done it with her, I didn't think she would have let him. I was a bit hurt because I thought I was his best friend and he never told me.

He kept on going on about his having hurt everybody and it all being his fault and he wouldn't listen to anything else. I was too tired to keep arguing with him and I was kind of pleased when the nurse told him that I had to rest.

Everything had started to hurt again so she came in and gave me something for the pain. I must have fallen asleep because mum was sitting there beside the bed when I opened my eyes.

She said she had spoken to Spider for a few minutes and he had been quite upset about me. I thought she would have been annoyed with him but I should have known better. Mum always says there is no use in making a fuss because it rarely solves anything. What's done is done. It's one of her favourite sayings.

She and dad had been by the bed when I came out of the anaesthetic last night. I kept on seeing them with wobbly lines around their bodies, and then they seemed to be floating. The next time I saw them they had pink spots above their heads, so I reckoned I was dreaming or something. One time I woke up and I was sure it was Fiona sitting by the bed. I almost called her name but then she looked up and it was mum.

I still don't know if I babbled while I was in that 'in and out' state. I hope I didn't. Mum and dad don't seem to be acting any differently so I suppose I never told them about Fiona. Sometimes I wish I had just told them the truth. Told them what really happened, that I had been the reason she fell. I had killed her.

I keep thinking about that day. When I got back round to the pond I couldn't see Fiona anywhere. I began to convince myself that she was all right, that in the time it took me to climb up to the top of the Hook and run back around to the pond, she must have stopped hiding and gone to look for me. I tried to convince myself, but I never really believed it.

Winter skeleton trees, some of them bent over almost to the water's edge, surrounded the ice-covered water of the pond. Everything was coated with a sprinkling of crystal white snow.

I scanned the pond trying to see her. I ran along the edge of the ice, ducking in and out of the trees and getting snow down my neck but I didn't care, until I got to the place we had crossed the pond.

I saw our footprints in the snow leading to where we had started our climb. I saw the dark shadow of the Hook on the ice, but I couldn't see anything else there.

I shouted, my voice raw and hoarse. "C'mon Fiona! Stop fooling about."

Silence.

I needed to get closer, to see into the shade below the rock face. The harsh glare of the ice was making my eyes smart as I stared across at the shadows trying to see, but not really wanting to.

I shivered as I stepped onto the ice, calling her name all the time. I followed our footprints towards the Hook but halfway there I heard a noise like a pistol shot.

The ice was cracking.

I stopped, frozen with terror.

I waited to see if the ice would crack beneath me and send me slipping down into the murky, frozen slime of the pond.

The pond surface was opaque and deceivingly solid. Our footprints were still clearly outlined in the thin feathery crust of snow lying on the icy surface.

The dark patch that I had thought was a shadow, now as I stared at it, was obviously a gash in the ice.

A bleached branch stuck out of the dark hole like a spear, rising at a strange angle above the ice. It formed itself into a recognisable limb, a white sleeve with a slim, pale hand.

Fiona.

The shock of seeing her arm sticking out of the ice made me feel suddenly weak. I sank down onto my knees, oblivious of the freezing cold and cracking ice. I called her name weakly but it emerged as a whisper. I couldn't find enough air to shout. I tried to shuffle closer to her but the ice started to make weird pistol-cracking noises again.

I can't remember how I got back to the edge of the pond and onto dry land. I think I shuffled along on my knees. Tears blinding my eyes and making frozen trails down my face, feeling as I turned back that once again I was abandoning her.

I ran to get help. I ran away from her in the other direction, leaving her there alone, down there in all that freezing water, with slimy weeds sticking to her hair.

I should have done something. I should have climbed back down the Hook instead of climbing further up, away from her. I should have been there to get her out of the icy water before she drowned.

I don't know what made me tell all those lies that day. When I ran to get help they were only concerned about trying to revive her. They told me how brave I was being and it was only much later that anyone started asking questions.

By then I had spoken to Joe, who was in the crowd of people watching them lift Fiona out of the water. I took him aside and swore him to secrecy.

"If anyone asks Fiona and I both stopped to speak to you then she went on to the pond on her own, right? I stayed and talked to you for a while."

I have always been a good bit taller and heavier than Joe, as well as being a year older. I put on the real 'Glasgow Heavy' act that always seems to give the younger kids the willies. Silly really, I've never hit anyone, not really. I think Joe's a bit scared of me but he also wants to come along with Spider and me and he knows I wouldn't let him if he grassed me up.

"Okay, Andy. You know I won't g..g..grass." He always stuttered when he was trying to convince me of anything.

So when the bizzies came and asked us all about it we both told the same story, that Fiona had gone off to the pond on her own while I was talking to Joe.

I told them that she had probably been climbing the Hook but when I arrived she had already fallen and I had tried all sorts of ways to get to her. I told them that the ice had started cracking so in the end I had to go and get help.

They all told me I was brave for trying so hard to save her and that I did the right thing otherwise I might have been drowned in the pond, too.

That only made it much worse because I knew that I had killed her. My foot had hit her face and knocked her off the Hook. If I had even climbed down after her I could have saved her.

Mum was just sitting there quietly but she smiled at me when she noticed my eyes were open.

"That nice policeman wants to come and speak to you, Andy," Mum said. The word 'police' jerked me back to the present with a nasty jolt.

"The police?" I mumbled, it was difficult to speak with all the bandages.

Mum nodded and continued knitting. She knits all the time, especially when she is worried about anything. When she gets really upset she knits even faster. This time I hoped she was only worried about my injuries, and not that the police were going to put me away for murder.

"That nice PC Hilton came along while you were in the operating theatre and said he would have to take a statement. He said he needs to speak to you about what happened last night."

It took me all of ten seconds to realise that if he had spoken to Mum while I was being operated on it couldn't have been because I had spilled the beans while coming around from the anaesthetic.

So it wasn't about Fiona, it was about the crash, and stealing the car. Maybe they were going to put me away for that instead.

"He said," Mum continued, "due to your injuries and all that they would probably be a bit easier on you, especially because you've only been up for this kind of thing once before. He thought that you had probably learnt your lesson, the hard way." Her voice choked up but she coughed and pretended it hadn't happened.

I tried to put Fiona out of my head. It wasn't about her; it was all about the crash.

"What about Spider?"

"Oh, I think he is in for a lot more trouble. PC Hilton told me that because Spider was driving Deanna's parents are determined to press charges, so it would be worse for him."

She shook her head. "I just don't understand why you did it at all. Look at you. You might have been…" Her mouth crimped up and the knitting needles were moving so fast they were almost a blur.

"I'm sorry, Mum. Really I am." I was about to start blubbing like a baby but I didn't care.

Everything hurts and I was so scared they had found out about Fiona that I had forgotten to ask what was going to happen to me. What I would look like when they took the bandages off my face. I don't want to think about that just now, so perhaps it's just as well I hadn't asked.

CHAPTER NINETEEN

Spider

The doors close on Hilton and Deanna's father and I sink down in the corner of the empty lift. I can't stop shaking. My head is thumping and I never want to get up again. The lift jolts to a stop on the next floor and when I look up I see there are two women waiting to get in. They look at me for a moment or two as I stagger painfully back to my feet.

One of them asks if I am all right and when I shrug my indifference she looks away as if embarrassed that she had bothered at all. I can see that they are trying not to make it obvious as they sneak looks at my bruises and my bandaged foot. They make faces to each other but I ignore them staring at the wall as if they don't exist.

The next floor is the ward where the nurse said I'd find Andy. I stumble out of the lift and I'm glad the corridor is quiet and empty. I need time to recover from the scene with Deanna's father. My head is still thumping and I feel sick and shaky.

I really thought he was going to go for me. It was only Hilton being there that stopped me being spread across the lift like jam.

I rest against the wall and lean my head back for a moment. A door opens and a doctor comes out so I move along to one of the long windows and stop beside it, leaning my head against the cool glass.

Deanna's father was always trying to keep us apart. Now it looks like he's after my blood. I wish I'd had the nerve to take him on, I knew I should have stood up to him and almost wished he'd taken a swing at me so that I would have had a reason to hit back. I really wanted to thump him, I want very badly to hit someone, anyone.

In reality I know that I would never hit Deanna's father. If I did she would probably never forgive me and he would have me up for assault as well, no doubt about that. So I would lose out on all sides, but I just wish...

I realise I am thumping my fist against the wall, and there are people walking along the corridor behind me, staring at me as they pass.

I start to walk towards Andy's ward. It takes a bit of persuading to get the ward sister to let me go in and see him but in the end she says I can have a few minutes.

She points to the door of a side ward. There are two old men and a third bed with the curtains drawn around it. I part them and slip inside. The curtains around his bed make it feel a bit more private. I am glad of that and that Andy has his eyes closed when I come in, so he doesn't see my face.

It looks like one of these silly horror films where the person's head is covered in bandages and it could be anyone at all underneath them. His name is above the bed so I know it's definitely Andy. He has his leg raised up under the covers as well. I swallow my fright as I remember what I had seen last night after the crash. I wonder what Andy is going to look like when all the bandages came off.

He opens his eyes and sees me.

"Hi, Andy. How you doing?" I ask, lamely, and then want to kick myself for saying such a stupid thing, but Andy doesn't seem to notice.

He croaks something then clears his throat and tries again. "Hi, Spider." His voice is muffled under the bandages. His words are slurred and I have to listen carefully to understand what he is saying. "You've got some bruises, eh? Looks like it was a good fight!"

His voice is rough but I can just make it out. He raises his bruised hand up to the bandages on his head. "The nurse says I look like the invisible man," he mumbles through split and bruised lips, the only skin I can see.

I try to look cheerful but my throat is thick and trying to choke me. What have I done to him; Andy, the joker. He is still joking even in this state. My best friend, since ever, now he's some strange broken invalid, and I did this to him. I can barely stand to look at him.

I stay and talk to Andy for a bit but he's finding it difficult to speak and I can't think of what to say except that I am sorry. Sorry I was driving; sorry we crashed; sorry because what I did ended up like this. But I can't even say the words. I want to get out but I can't just walk out on him, so I am relieved when the nurse comes in and says I should let him rest.

I head out of the ward not noticing anything, too wrapped up in my head when I hear a voice call my name.

"Spider? Is that you?"

I whirl around and my stomach catapults to my boots like a giant boulder. Andy's mum is standing there, smiling at me! She looks thin and pale, and she has dark smudges under her eyes as if she hasn't slept for a long time.

I swallow a couple of times. For some reason her smiling is worse than all the accusations in the world. Makes me feel even worse; bad enough that she has already lost her daughter but now I have almost killed her son.

I stumble over a few words and make a lame excuse that they are waiting for me back in the ward downstairs. She accepts the lie with a warm smile, telling me to come back and see Andy soon.

I feel bad about rushing away from her. I could have stood another argument with Deanna's father, rather than Andy's mum being nice to me.

She's a good sort, Andy's mum. Always has been, and I should know, I've been going round to their house ever since they moved here from Glasgow. When things at our house were at their worst I could always sneak off to Andy's and his mum would make a fuss of me. Not that they had much more than we did, Andy's dad had been too ill to work for years, but their house was quiet and happy. No one shouted and yelled at each other.

It made it all even more horrible when Fiona died. I kind of liked Fiona, she was feisty and was always trying to prove that she could do things better than Andy. When she drowned all the happiness seemed to disappear from Andy's house. He never wanted to be at home. After that I hardly ever went there any more, so I hadn't seen Andy's mum for a long time.

I need to get away on my own; to make some sense of what is happening, to get it all straight in my head.

But first I have to see Deanna.

CHAPTER TWENTY

Spider

I head back out of the ward. I need to see Deanna but I hope her father isn't there. What happened in the lift scared me shitless and meeting Andy's mum was just about as bad, in a different way. I'm becoming a real wimp. I don't know what's wrong with me. I never used to feel like this. Maybe Deanna's father is right I'm useless and no good to anybody. I can't even stand up for myself.

The ward isn't very busy so I just walk in and peer through the small windows set high in the doors to see if she is in one of the side rooms. The third one has three empty beds in it and one person in the fourth bed.

It's Deanna.

I push open the door and slip in.

"Spider!" Her face is bruised and swollen and there's a large plaster across her right temple. She gives me a lopsided smile.

"Deanna. Are you okay?"

I try not to limp too much as I move over to the bed and sit on the edge of it. Deanna reaches out her arms and draws me into a tight hug. I hold her gently, frightened to hurt her, she looks so fragile.

"Oh, Spider." I could see she was trying not to cry but the tears just flooded from her eyes. "I'm sorry," she gulps. "I didn't want to start crying again."

"It's all right, Deanna. It's going to be all right." I feel helpless.

I never know what to do when someone starts to cry. "It'll be all right. Really it will."

"I'm sorry, Spider. I knew you didn't want to go on a Run again. Now you'll get into all kinds of trouble and it was all my fault!"

"No way! It wasn't your fault. I could have said no, Deanna. I didn't have to do it. Anyway I was the one who was driving when we crashed and everyone got hurt. I didn't ever mean this to happen."

We sit holding each other for a few moments. Deanna holds onto me as if she doesn't want to let go but then she pushes away, gently. She looks scared as if she isn't sure of me. I've never seen Deanna like this, she is usually so sure of herself.

"Spider, there's something I have to tell you," she begins.

I put my finger on her lips to silence her. "I know about the baby. Why didn't you tell me?"

She is trying hard to hold back another deluge of tears. She has never been one of those girls who cried at everything. She always says she hates girls like that. When she speaks it all comes out in a rush.

"I was so frightened. I didn't know what you would say. I thought you might be annoyed and not want to see me any more. I'm so sorry." The tears stream down her face. "I didn't tell anyone, I was so scared my parents would find out and I didn't know what to do. It was horrible, Spider."

"You should have told me. I would have taken care of you, no matter what your parents said."

I feel even worse now, knowing how worried she must have been and that she didn't think she could trust me to be there for her.

"It was my baby, too," I tell her. "I would have been a good father, really I would."

Deanna puts her hand up and strokes my hair back, out of my eyes. "I know you would." She buries her face in my shoulder. It feels right. For the first time since the accident I feel calm and at peace.

With a crash the door bursts open.

"What the Hell do you think you're doing here?" Deanna's father's voice startles us apart. "Get out of here, you little bastard," he roars, striding towards me. "Don't you think you've caused enough damage already? Get away from my daughter."

"Dad, don't!" Deanna pleads, but her father ignores her, his face a mask of rage.

I stand up beside the bed, shielding Deanna as if her father is dangerous and might attack her. I have faced my own father down but this is entirely different, Deanna's father is no unsteady drunk but a well-built, fit man fuelled by anger.

"I'm going to see that you get put away where you can't harm anyone else ever again. I should beat you to a pulp, here and now. She was a sweet innocent girl until you came along and destroyed all that. I should..." His fists clench and unclench as he tries to control himself. "You almost killed her you little...."

"Dad, please," Deanna implores him in a small desperate voice.

Her father hold his arms tightly at his side as if he doesn't trust himself to move them in case he lets rip with the murder that is in his eyes.

I swallow and try to stand straighter as he moves threateningly close and stares me down. I have no idea what Deanna's father might do but I'm not about to let him send me away.

Deanna is holding on to my hand, squeezing it tightly.

"Paul!"

Deanna's mother has come into the room behind him. "Paul, don't!" She walks up to her husband and places her hand on his arm. "Paul," she says again, quietly and firmly.

For a moment the tension almost makes the air sizzle and then all his fury seems to subside. He turns away and walks to the window, standing staring out at nothing, not moving at all.

"Now, I think you should go, Spider," she says in a cool and steady voice. "You are in enough trouble already."

I nod slowly and turn to Deanna. "I'll come back to see you." I clasp her hand tightly and mouth the words.

Deanna looks up with tears in her eyes. "Oh, Spider," she whispers helplessly.

There is nothing either of us can do.

I have to leave.

CHAPTER TWENTY-ONE

Spider

I stumble out of the ward.

All I can think about is how frail and bruised Deanna looks. I never meant her to get hurt. I don't even know if she blames me, she would be right if she did. It is all my fault. She was so upset when she talked about the baby. I wanted to talk about it some more. I wanted to talk to her, to tell her how I felt, how I wished I hadn't been driving the car so fast.

I got off the lightest. I wish I had been killed. That would have been better than having to see her and Andy in such a mess, knowing I had caused it.

My fault! My fault! The words roar in my head.

I step back into the lift and press the top button. I can't face going back to the ward just now, I need some space, a place to think, to get away from all the voices and noise in my head.

If I go down to the ward my Dad might be there and he is the last person I want to see. I can just see his face as he was last night, all twisted up with some kind of perverse pleasure as he tells me yet again how stupid I am. I can hear him in my head as clearly as if he is standing in front of me.

"What kind of a stupid little bugger are you anyway? You get all that from your mother's side, just like your uncle Gary, always thieving and trying to be the great 'I am'. Trying to prove you are better than everyone else. Where do you think you get off, going about with a tart like that? They're all the same, and it doesn't make a bit of difference with all her airs and graces and fancy money, they're all the same underneath. You're a useless little bugger."

He never missed a chance to throw his prejudice in my face. He was working class and proud of it and he couldn't see anything about Deanna except that she was rich. God knows what he would say if he found out she had been pregnant. He would probably never have survived it because I would have gone for him, whatever he said.

Weird, how both our fathers were in some ways the same. The last thing Deanna's father probably wanted for her was to be going with someone like me. He probably wanted her to get together with some rich boy, so I suppose it wouldn't matter what I did, he would never want me near her.

I suppose I don't really have much going for me anyway, especially now. Hilton's not said too much but I know I'll be sent away for this one, there's no doubt about that. There's no way Deanna's father would let her near someone with a prison record.

I've heard all the stories about prison, too, who hasn't? I'm not sure I could do with being locked up for months or years even… shit! Locked away for years. Oh, shit…it's too much to get my head around.

The lift doors open and I wander out into the corridor. For a moment I have no idea where I am, then I remember I had pushed the button for the top floor. At least I'm not likely to meet anyone I know up here.

It's a bit busier than I had expected and I limp along trying to ignore the people passing by. They all seem to be looking at me, staring, and I just want to get away from them. I have to get away. I need to find somewhere quiet, somewhere I can rest for a bit and get it all straight in my head with no one telling me what to do or what I had done.

"Are you all right, son?"

I try to ignore the voice but it's a nurse who is suddenly standing in front of me. She seems to be waiting for me to look up at her.

"I'm fine," I mumble and try to get past her.

"Are you lost? What ward are you looking for?"

"I'm fine!" I shout at her and push past. I don't want to talk to anyone. I know she's still watching me as I hobble off so I go through the next set of double doors and keep on walking. I have no idea where I am going but I don't care anyway. My foot has started to ache badly but the pain gets lost in the mess that is my head, along with the all other aches and confusion.

I have to find somewhere to get away from everyone. I start looking in the windows of the doors as I pass them. Most of them have beds with people in them. I have to find somewhere quiet soon or I will crack up.

There are only two doors left. I look behind me and see that there is no one watching. I check again but the room is empty, I can see that much through the small window in the grey door. I turn the handle, push open the door and escape from the corridor. Away from the disapproving faces that scowl at me as I limp past. Away from the uniforms and white coats.

The sterile, smell that pervades the entire building is echoed in the plain, sanitized room. The covers on the bed are thin and tightly folded over, more like cardboard than a comfortable place to rest. The walls are an endless blank expanse that disappears behind the dull yellow curtains at the side of the bed. I want to mess it all up, cover the walls with graffiti, muss up the bedcovers. My head is too full, too chaotic to stand all this ordered neatness. Full of anger and hatred all raging inside me, filling my head until it wants to burst.

It's all my fault. Andy, Deanna, I almost killed them like I killed the baby. Our baby, what kind of useless father had I turned out to be?

I stumble across the room towards the window trying to escape the explosion of competing voices in my head.

I press my forehead against the glass and close my eyes. A strange noise echoes across the empty room, it 's coming from me. I'm gasping for breath. The room feels unbearably hot and airless.

The paint on the window is old and flaking off in places, exposing the soft splintered wood beneath. I force the catch open with my thumb and try to pull up the window from the bottom, but it's stuck. Now that I have a reason to use it, my anger gives me strength and I push against the top bar of the window; jerk it, watching the old paint crack along the sill. Another surge of effort and it reluctantly screeches open. I lean out and gulp in the cool air as if I had been holding my breath for hours.

It's a long way down.

I lean further out, past a narrow ledge that runs just below the window. The familiar scary tingle in my arms and hands flashes through my entire body, as my fear of heights asserts its claim. Like fingering a wound to see how bad the pain is, I tease the sensation by leaning further over. My stomach tumbles, but a small voice inside urges me farther than I want to go.

Without any memory of how I got here I am sitting astride the window ledge, one leg dangling over the drop. The laces of my trainers, loose to accommodate the bandage, dangle freely below my foot like wriggling streamers, hanging down above the dizzy space. I dip my head under the window. My head and shoulders are now outside.

A light rain has started. It's cool on my face. I watch the curtain of raindrops falling on the grey roof tiles of the next building; on the window ledge beside me; out in the space between.

Falling down…down…down….to the road below, darkening the surface and making it slick and wet.

I lift my other leg over the sill and perch precariously on the thin outer window edge, both feet dangling into the open air. A streaming river of electric shivers tingles along the nerves of my arms and on to the tips of my fingers. My stomach is churning, greasy and sickening.

Part of me is screaming to go back inside but I turn around almost as if someone else is in control, pushing me on. Gripping the windowsill I let myself slip, my feet scuffing against the wall towards the narrow ledge below. The toes of my trainers scrape down the wall. It seems to go on forever, much further than I had thought. For a moment I panic that I have somehow missed the ledge. A vision of falling, of plummeting to the ground, sends painful shocks to my palms and I almost let go.

My toes touch the ledge.

I edge along until I reach the far end of the windowsill. There is a wider sill just across the gap, an arm's length away with a drainpipe rising up the wall in between. If I can reach the next windowsill I should be able to step over to the flat roof beyond.

A shout down below makes me stop. I look down, over my shoulder and I can see the car park. Someone has seen me up here on the ledge and they are shouting for help. Why can't they just mind their own business?

I want to be alone.

I want time to think, to get it all straight in my head.

Reaching out, I grab the drainpipe and it shudders as I touch it, threatening to come away from the wall. I tug at it, but it stays firm so I grab it and edge my feet along the ledge, closer to the pipe. As I grab the pipe with both hands it shudders again. If it comes loose now nothing would stop me plunging to the ground. I shiver, imagining for a moment that I am falling, my body dropping, arms and legs flailing around as I fall.

My foot knocks against the pipe as I try to step around it, almost making me let go of my handhold. I find the ledge on the other side of the pipe, first with one foot, and then the other. I reach out and grab for the security of the wider windowsill beyond the pipe. I can feel my fingernails splitting as they try to bite into the stone. My heart feels like bursting, I can hardly breathe. I let go of the drainpipe, sending crumbling bits of metal spiralling down through the air to the waiting concrete below. For a moment I am with them, floating in dizzying curves, a mote of human debris.

With a thud my heart brings me back. I edge along the wall and throw myself the last step onto the flat roof. The landing jars my bruised ribs and a knife-like pain shoots through my ankle as it gives way, making me stagger and fall onto my knees, but a wave of relief floods through me.

Now I can see the circus that is developing down below. Someone has called the bizzies and I can hear their sirens as they approach the hospital. There is an ambulance there already and a large group of people staring up at me. They look like demented ants as they mill around, hoping to see something, some spectacle.

Will I jump or will I fall?

I don't care what they think.

Will I end up smashed up on the concrete? Suddenly all I can think about is Andy, the blood, smashed bone and torn flesh; it didn't even look like a face anymore. I don't deserve to have friends.

I don't deserve to live. I'm a murderer.

I might as well step out into the void. It's the only solution.

The ground is just a step…

and a long drop away…

to oblivion.

CHAPTER TWENTY-TWO

When Davey Hilton finally arrived back down at the ward to collect him, he was told that Spider wasn't there. One of the nurses thought he had gone home but she wasn't sure. Hilton turned and was about to leave when he decided to stop and ask her to check and make sure.

She came back a few moments later looking a little embarrassed.

"I'm sorry, you were right, he hasn't gone home yet. As far as I can make out he's somewhere in the hospital. Staff said he had gone to visit some friends of his on another ward but he's not come back down here, yet."

"Right. Perhaps you could make sure he waits for me when he gets back here?" Hilton asked her. "I'll go upstairs and see if I can track him down. I have a fair idea where he'll be."

He was leaving the ward when a commotion started up behind him. A porter had rushed past him into the ward bursting with news, and whatever he had to say was making quite an impression on the nurses. Hilton was about to ignore it when a sixth sense made him turn around and inquire as to the cause of all the excitement.

"We've got a 'Jumper'! He's on the roof," the porter told him, with a kind of excited glee.

Hilton stared at the man for a moment, his brain processing the information and making snap connections on an instinctive level. He didn't know why but he was sure he knew who it was. He had to get up there, and fast.

"Where exactly is he?" he asked the porter.

Keen to impart all of his meagre knowledge, the porter was only too happy to offer his services. "On the top floor. I can take you there."

Hilton was reluctant to take observers, but at least he would get there quickly. "Okay. Let's go!"

He cursed himself for not foreseeing this whole scenario. He realised he should have known that Spider was close to the edge.

On the 7th floor a crowd had gathered outside the door of one of the side wards. Hilton elbowed his way into the room, his police uniform giving him the right to push in unquestioned.

"What's going on?" he asked one of the men who was hovering by the window.

"A kid's climbed out onto the roof. He looks like he's about to jump." The man peered through the glass and shook his head dismally. "It's one hell of a way down."

Hilton leaned out of the window. It was a long drop down to the ground where a crowd swarmed around the car park like vultures, eager for blood and spectacle. He had never understood why people rushed forward to see grim horror and then complained about how ghastly it was.

There was a buzz of excitement in the room and it

sickened him. Hilton turned back to the porter who had followed in his wake and was trying to peer over his shoulder to see out the window.

"Try to clear this room, would you?" Hilton knew the man would delight in the momentary power. Within moments the room was empty apart from himself and the porter.

"Is there another way onto that roof?" Hilton asked him.

After a moment's consideration the man shook his head. "Not that I know of. All the windows are on the other side."

Hilton sighed as he leaned out of the window. A narrow ledge led to a small flat area of roof with nothing but a small skylight breaking the smooth surface and it was far too small to climb through. Standing peering over the edge at the crowd on the street below was a tall, thin figure he recognised.

"Spider!"

Hilton watched as the boy looked back at him, a strange look flashing across his face, but Hilton wasn't sure what it was, anger, guilt, frustration? He had no time to worry about it, he felt as though the last minutes of Spider's life were running through his fingers like sand and he wasn't sure he could do anything to halt them.

He had no training for this kind of thing but he was the one who was there. He knew Spider and there was no way he was going to let him throw away his life without doing something.

He hoped the boy would say something, anything,

to help him to judge his state of mind. It was quite a distance from the window to the far side of the roof and Hilton knew he would have to get closer but he was trying to think of another way around it. He was trying to convince himself that he might be able to persuade Spider to come back in without going out onto the roof with him. It looked like the only way to get there was by climbing out of the window and Hilton couldn't even think about the drop below him without feeling his head spinning.

What could he say to the boy? He thought of several things then discarded them all as stupid and more likely to promote the wrong kind of response. He tried something fairly neutral.

"Can we talk?"

Spider shrugged.

Hilton opened the window wider and sat on the edge. Even that made him queasy.

"You could come back in and we could have a talk about it."

Spider shook his head and shrugged casually. "No point."

Hilton took a deep breath and swung his feet over the windowsill.

"What're you doing?" Spider asked. He hadn't moved from his laid back position but his face became more animated.

"I'm not sure." Hilton really wasn't sure what he was doing but he didn't seem to have much choice in the matter. "Is this the way you came out?"

Spider nodded.

He seemed interested now, waiting to see just what Hilton would do, a kind of challenge.

Hilton looked at the ledge below and the distance to the safety of the flat roof. He kept his eyes well averted from the dizzying drop. A little voice inside was screaming at him to get back inside but one look at Spider and he knew he was going to ignore it. The perverse side of his nature hated abandoning a challenge. Cursing himself for his own stupidity he turned over onto his stomach and shinned down the wall until his feet touched the ledge.

CHAPTER TWENTY-THREE

Spider

It's the only real solution. Everybody will be happier with me out of the way. With all the terrible things I've caused, Andy's face and the nightmares of what he has in front of him, operations and scars. Will he ever look the same again?

Deanna, all bruised and broken; and then there's the baby. I would have been a father, me! I know I wouldn't have been like my old man; I'd have been a good father. But the baby is gone and there isn't much chance that I'll be allowed to see Deanna again. As far as her father is concerned I got her pregnant and almost killed her. No way he is going to let her anywhere near me again.

There's no other way.

Everyone will be better off with me out of the way.

It is so much simpler now that I've worked it all through in my head with no one around to mess it all up again.

Life should be simpler but people keep on trying to make things complicated. It's not so scary standing here on the edge of the roof, when I don't care if I fall or jump off. It looks so easy, just one step into the air and everything will go away. I can almost imagine the feeling of flying through the air.

Why not?

Then Hilton pokes his head out of the window.

He says he wants to talk. Not a lot of point but I'm not in any hurry, I can jump anytime I want. Hilton looks terrified as he stares down at the road below. I know how he feels. I thought he would just sit there and make conversation, try to talk me out of it. Instead he turns around and starts climbing out of the window.

It is almost scarier watching him climb along the ledge than it had been doing it myself. I can see he is nervous, the sweat is pouring off him after a few minutes and he keeps trying to shake it out of his eyes.

I wonder if he is going to make it past the drainpipe. He stops halfway with one foot on either side. I think his nerve has given out. It seems like forever before he moves again, shuffling his foot along the side nearest to me until he is spread-eagled across the wall. Finally he manages to get his other hand across.

By the time he gets to the flat roof beside me his face is pure white with bright red burning spots on his cheeks. He sits there mopping up the sweat from his face and neck, panting like a steam engine on full throttle.

There is a round of applause from the crowd below. What did they have to do with it? All they wanted was something exciting to watch, why don't they go home and put on the TV and watch one of those documentaries or something?

I reckon he's a good sort, Hilton. Going out on that ledge just so as he could get up here to talk me out of jumping. Could have told him not to bother, that it's a waste of time. I know I wouldn't have risked my neck for some stupid kid like me.

It won't do any good, anyhow, no matter what he says, but he's got some bottle, so I suppose I should let him have a go.

"Pretty hairy climb that," he says, once he's got his breath back.

I shrug. He wants to talk so I let him get on with it.

"I never liked heights, really. Even when I was a kid I hated going on all those high rides, wall of death sort of thing." He stops suddenly. It's almost comical. I can almost see him thinking, 'Bugger, I shouldn't have mentioned death!'

"What's it all about, Spider?"

He stands up and wanders closer to the edge of the roof and looks over. I can see he is trying to be blasé about it but he stays a few feet from the edge and comes away again pretty quickly.

"Trying to make a statement, or do you really want to throw yourself off?" He raises his eyebrows at me. "Make quite a mess of yourself if you land down there."

I shrug again. Did he really think this was going to make any difference?

"I don't suppose that would bother you, but have you thought about what would happen if you jumped and didn't kill yourself? Spending the rest of your life unable to walk or move about without someone doing it for you? Not able to go for a pee without help?"

Woa! That was nasty. No way would anyone survive that kind of a fall is there? He's just kidding me on. Well, I'm not about to let him talk me out if it. No way.

He can see that he has shaken me because he gives that small grim smile I've seen before. He leans back against the roof, well away from the edge. "It's happened before, Spider. I'm not making it up."

I am beginning to wish he would go away and let me jump in peace. All he is doing is making things complicated again.

"I don't care," I lie.

"What about Andy?" Hilton just doesn't know when to leave well alone. "He needs you now, Spider. You're Andy's best friend. Don't you think he needs to know you are there for him, with all the operations he's to go through?"

"I'd not see him anyway, if I was in prison."

"But he would know you were there. You could write to him. And Deanna. How is she going to feel? She's lost that baby. It doesn't matter to her that it was hardly any size at all, that she hadn't known for very long. Women feel about these things much more because it is happening inside them She will feel she's lost something very dear to her, she won't want to lose you, too. How is she going to cope with the thought of you killing yourself? She might feel it was her fault. Is that what you want?"

"She probably blames me for everything anyway," I hiss though clenched teeth. I know that isn't true but I say it anyway. "I killed our baby. Almost killed Andy too,"

I turn away and look over the edge.

I can sense him sitting up and tensing behind me. I realise he thinks I am about to jump.

Why not? Might as well get it over with. Too bad if I survive, at least everyone would feel sorry for me then.

He starts on about his own kids and how he knows my dad is a bit of a bastard but I have a life ahead of me, a chance to turn it around in the future.

I'm not really listening. His voice is like a buzz of noise at the back of my head. I watch the people down below. The bizzies have put up a cordon around the foot of the building and are keeping the people back behind it. There are all sorts of vans and trucks down there. I might even be on TV, strange how even that

doesn't seem to matter.
  Nothing matters anymore.
  It's so easy.
  One small step....

CHAPTER TWENTY-FOUR

Andy

In the last three days I've had two operations and today everything hurts. I had a long talk with the doctor about my face and I have to admit I am a bit scared of the whole business. They warned me that it wasn't going to look very good for a while but the surgeon thought he should be able to make me look what he called 'passing normal', but it will take a while.

I almost didn't ask what he meant but he was really easy-going and I'm glad I did. He's Australian and has a great sense of humour; you probably have to have with his job.

He said he meant that by the time all the scars had settled and calmed down and if I didn't cut my hair too short, most people who passed me in the street wouldn't notice the scars.

He said that up close I would have some scars but he said I would look rakish, not sure what that means but I think it is something about looking like I was streetwise.

He did warn me that it would be a while before I got to that stage, and I had a long road of operations and skin grafts ahead.

Being in the hospital means spending a lot more time with mum and dad. They've been in almost all the time. Strange I don't think I've ever had so much time with them. Mum started talking about Fiona last night.

She said she knew something was bothering me about how she died. Both of us ended up in tears but in the end I told her what had actually happened. She didn't look horrified or anything.

"It was an accident, Andy," she said. "You weren't responsible, there was nothing you could have done to stop her from falling."

"But I didn't climb down when she fell! I just stayed there, I couldn't move. Even when I did move, I climbed up instead and that meant I had to go all the way round. It took me ages and when I got there…it was too late." I could hardly whisper the words.

Mum shook her head. "It wouldn't have made any difference. Fiona hit her head when she fell in. There was nothing you could have done. If you had climbed down the ice would have cracked under you and we would have lost you too." Mum gripped my hand tightly her eyes bright and full of tears.

"It's all in the past now. We have to go on." She took out a tissue and mopped her eyes.

I couldn't believe how long I had worried about it and wished I'd had spoken to her before about it. If only I'd said something. I had been carrying that blame for such a long time. Thinking that Mum and dad would blame me, too.

Perhaps I should have let Fiona go first, or persuaded her not to do the climb. I might have talked her out of it, but then perhaps not, knowing Fiona.

Then there was the news about Spider. I hadn't believed it at first and I just kept on saying, 'No way!'

Part of me still can't believe it, not Spider.

He was always so confident, so in control, why would he want to kill himself? I imagine him standing on the roof fearless as always.

Or was he?

How had he felt all alone on that roof wanting to end it all. He must have been on some huge guilt trip about what had happened to Deanna and me. I wish I'd been there. That's what friends are for, stopping you doing that kind of thing. Spider would have been there for me if I was the one on the roof. He'd have talked me out of it and told me not to be so stupid. He was always the one who knew what to do, had all the ideas. He was always there, we were best mates, but I wasn't there for Spider when he needed me.

What am I going to do without him around to hang out with?

CHAPTER TWENTY-FIVE

Deanna

Spider...I can't even say his name without crying.

How did he feel up there on that roof? He must have been so alone and miserable to do something like that.

I cried all day after Andy told me.

I was so angry that no one had said anything about Spider that I refused to even speak to my parents when they came in.

I couldn't stop crying.

How could they be so insensitive? They don't seem to think I have any real feelings that I'm too young to know what I want and what I feel.

I miss him so much already.

Andy was quite sweet to me. He said that Spider had told him about the baby and everything. He told me not to think it was my fault.

At first I wouldn't believe it. Spider was so confident; he never seemed to let anything bother him at all. My parents must have known all about what happened but they didn't say anything, even when I asked about him.

Well, I asked my mum. Dad would have gone ballistic if I had even mentioned Spider to him.

Spider

I told Andy what had happened between my dad and Spider and I realised that was probably one of the things that drove him up onto the roof in the first place.

Andy looks in a terrible mess and he must have seen the shock on my face when I first went in to see him. But it's strange, after talking to him for a few minutes I had forgotten how he looked and it was just the usual Andy except that we probably got on better than we ever had before. He wasn't as funny as he usually is, but that's not surprising.

Andy's going to be in and out of hospital for months, getting his face fixed so I promised I would come in and see him.

They tell me I can leave hospital today, after the consultant has finished speaking to Mum and Dad. At first they thought I might have had some kind of lasting effect from banging my head and they had to strap up my wrist again, where it was sprained, now that the swelling had calmed down. I look a bit of a sight. All the bruises on my face have come out in gaudy colours. I have bits that are purple and a sickly yellowish browny-green.

I wish I could have seen Spider again, even just for a few minutes. There are so many things I wanted to say to him.

CHAPTER TWENTY-SIX

Correspondence from Andy's Home for the totally weird

Thursday

Hi Deanna,

I'm writing this on the laptop they gave me to do my school work while I'm in hospital. It's pretty neat and I can even get it to play a few games.

Thought I'd write you because I'm stuck in hospital again for the next few days. Had my seventh operation yesterday, but hey, who's counting! This last operation was just a small one and I am feeling better already.

They say it is all going well but I think I still look a bit strange, although it is amazing what you get used to. I found a photo of me last week, taken before the crash. Mum and dad had hidden most of our photos away, they think I don't know but I overheard them talking about it ages ago. So it was a bit of a surprise seeing how I used to look. I had almost forgotten, well, probably not really. People still stare a lot, especially just after an op when the scars are still sore looking. Anyway they say I only have a few more to go and that should be it.

So, how's it going at that fancy boarding school of yours? Strange to think it's been almost a year now. I got your emails. Sounds from your last one that you are enjoying it a bit more now. Hope the end of year exams weren't as bad as you thought they were going to be! I'm sure a brain like you got top marks anyway.

Have you decided what university you're applying for? Can't believe you are going to Australia for the summer holidays. You jammy thing! When do you leave?

Guess what? I've got a place on that film and media course I told you about. It starts in September. They are going to let me have time off for my operations and say I can take work away to do in hospital if I need to. I can't wait.

My other great news is that I heard from Spider. He's getting out tomorrow. Can't believe how time has flown and that he's been banged up for a year. He didn't want to go and stay at home, I think his dad has pretty much said he's not welcome and anyway I don't think Spider wants to see him, either. So he's coming to stay with us for a little while, so that he can go and see his mum and the rest of the family.

I hate to admit it but I feel a bit weird about seeing him again after all this time. I wonder how much he's changed? Not sure, either, what he's going to think about the way I look now.

Anyway I'll let you know how it goes.

Bye for now,

Andy

CHAPTER TWENTY-SEVEN

Spider

In the end I never could remember what Hilton said that made me start to think about not jumping. Perhaps part of it was because he was willing to climb out onto the ledge beside me, I saw how scared he was, and he could have stayed inside. No one has ever cared that much about what happened to me.

I told Andy I'd been bored by all the rubbish the man had been going on about, and had come down just to get some peace! But I think he knew that was just my way of making it less heavy.

I've not really been in touch with Deanna very much. I wanted to write to her but somehow I never found the right words. She and Andy have been swapping emails and sometimes he tells me about her in his letters.

I still get the same nightmares about the crash, although not so often now. At first I thought I wouldn't ever want to drive again, at least not for a long while, anyway, but now I think I might. But who knows what I will feel like when I get out.

I used to think I could do anything, get away with anything.

I thought I was invincible...

But I wasn't.

❖ ❖ ❖

Today's the day. Can't really believe it but everyone keeps re-minding me. Strange, but now it's time to leave here the outside world seems a bit scarier than I thought it would. I've spent so much time planning and thinking about what it will be like to be getting ready to be outside again and it feels nothing like I thought it would.

I'll have to pull myself together. This is crazy. It's probably this place. You begin to lose your identity after a while.

Andy's parents said I can go and stay with them for a few days so that I can see Mum and the kids before I go off to start the mechanics course Donald, my social worker, organised for me.

No way I am ever coming back in here again.

Every time I think of how close I was to getting a much lon-ger sentence, it makes me shudder. When the lawyer said that if Deanna's baby had been a few weeks older I would have been had up for manslaughter, I just stared at him in disbelief.

That was how I had felt about the baby, anyway, but to hear him say it out loud was so much worse. Just as well I didn't hear him say that before I went up onto the hospital roof or nothing would have stopped me from jumping.

It could have easily been Deanna and Andy who were dead as well. That kept me up for nights in cold sweats and nightmares. When I first came in here there were loads of times I wished I had gone ahead and jumped.

I remember when they shut the door that first night. I was an-gry and, to be honest, shit scared. I was so lonely and empty. It all seemed pointless.

Some of the others here swagger about as though they couldn't give a damn. I don't believe any of them. Like the new boy who arrived last week. I can see him ending up back here within days of getting out, if he ever gets out in the first place. He's already got days added to his sentence after the stunt he tried yesterday.

I did that too for a bit, and got myself into bother more than once. Almost ended up with the wrong crowd before I realised that they were maniacs and it wasn't worth it.

I'd probably have been out last week except for the punishment days that were added on from the first couple of weeks. Once I saw that there were benefits to going along with the system I started working on the rehab project. I always knew I liked cars but I never would have thought I could fix other machines. Donald says I have a natural instinct for fault finding, especially when I managed to get the boilers fixed that freezer of a day last winter when even the bloke they called in to fix it couldn't see what was wrong.

That was a good day.

Deanna wrote to me a couple of times, just after her parents sent her off to boarding school. But it was never going to last, not after what happened.

I sometimes think about what it would have been like if we'd never gone on that Run. We came so close to blitzing ourselves that it changed us into different people. You can't go through that and stay the same.

Sometimes I used to think about what it would have been like if Deanna had had the baby, but there's no point in that. Her parents would probably never have let her have it or they would have made her give it up for adoption or something, I suppose. And then there's Andy. He sounds very positive but he's still having operations on his face. I can't imagine what he looks like now. Will I even recognise him? He says he looks different, but not too scary.

One of the things about being in here meant I never had to face any of that. But today I'll have to see Andy and that shakes me to my bones.

Hilton said he'd come and collect me. He didn't have to, he's moved on now and been promoted, he's a Sergeant, in Traffic. Spends his time stopping folk like me from racing on the roads, I suppose.

Good bloke, though, Hilton. I can't get rid of the picture of him climbing out of that window, his face a mask of terror as he looked at how far he might fall. He's got bottle.

One last check under the bed in case I've left anything. Seems like a small case to take everything I have in the world. Wish I could stop that sick feeling in my guts. Just nerves I suppose.

Damn sure I'm not coming back to this place. As Donald always says, it's my choice and my life so it's up to me what I do with it.

That sounds like them coming to get me now.

"Yeah, I'm ready."